wm gw

USA TODAY BESTSELLING AUTHOR
Dale Mayer

Steven's
SOLACE

HEROES FOR HIRE

D1212578

STEVEN'S SOLACE: HEROES FOR HIRE, BOOK 29
Beverly Dale Mayer
Valley Publishing Ltd.

Copyright © 2023

ISBN-13: 978-1-773367-74-3
Print Edition

Books in This Series:

Levi's Legend: Heroes for Hire, Book 1

Stone's Surrender: Heroes for Hire, Book 2

Merk's Mistake: Heroes for Hire, Book 3

Rhodes's Reward: Heroes for Hire, Book 4

Flynn's Firecracker: Heroes for Hire, Book 5

Logan's Light: Heroes for Hire, Book 6

Harrison's Heart: Heroes for Hire, Book 7

Saul's Sweetheart: Heroes for Hire, Book 8

Dakota's Delight: Heroes for Hire, Book 9

Tyson's Treasure: Heroes for Hire, Book 10

Jace's Jewel: Heroes for Hire, Book 11

Rory's Rose: Heroes for Hire, Book 12

Brandon's Bliss: Heroes for Hire, Book 13

Liam's Lily: Heroes for Hire, Book 14

North's Nikki: Heroes for Hire, Book 15

Anders's Angel: Heroes for Hire, Book 16

Reyes's Raina: Heroes for Hire, Book 17

Dezi's Diamond: Heroes for Hire, Book 18

Vince's Vixen: Heroes for Hire, Book 19

Ice's Icing: Heroes for Hire, Book 20

Johan's Joy: Heroes for Hire, Book 21

Galen's Gemma: Heroes for Hire, Book 22

Zack's Zest: Heroes for Hire, Book 23

Bonaparte's Belle: Heroes for Hire, Book 24

Noah's Nemesis: Heroes for Hire, Book 25

Tomas's Trials: Heroes for Hire, Book 26

Carson's Choice: Heroes for Hire, Book 27

Dante's Decision: Heroes for Hire, Book 28

Steven's Solace: Heroes for Hire, Book 29

Heroes for Hire, Books 1–3

Heroes for Hire, Books 4–6

Heroes for Hire, Books 7–9

Heroes for Hire, Books 10–12

Heroes for Hire, Books 13–15

Heroes for Hire, Books 16–18

Heroes for Hire, Books 19–21

Heroes for Hire, Books 22–24

About This Book

Finding out that an old friend was kidnapped, tortured, then deep-sixed in the harbor, complete with cement boots—and survived—sends Steven rushing to California to help. Also Opal and her mother had appealed to Levi to find Steven and to send him to help, if possible.

Opal has been through the worst possible scenario, but it's not over, as her kidnapers were looking for something she didn't have. She'd been to hell and back for a couple years already and had hoped the worst was over. How wrong could she be? And it wouldn't ever end, unless she found what these men were looking for or stopped them altogether.

With her in hiding, and Steven now back in her life, she's finally hopeful she might survive. Until things take an ugly turn, … and having a future is no longer a guarantee.

Prologue

W HEN TYSON WALKED into the kitchen of Levi's compound the next morning, he looked over at Levi and said, "You're running a pretty good streak."

"Not only that, I have a good chance at getting them both to work for me too." Levi rubbed his hands together.

"You know that you'll almost need a bigger place. You've got so many on your team."

"Thankfully those two are likely to stay where they are, at least until her son graduates."

"Which is only a few months from now," he reminded Levi.

"Right. It is only a few months, isn't it? But still, that's down the road, and I've got a very strange job next."

"It seems like all we've had lately are strange jobs."

"They're good for testing the new guys," he noted. "We've got so many ops in progress all over the place right now. We've even got a four-man team helping Bullard. I do have a simpler case, but that's off in California."

"What is the job?"

Just then Steven walked in, interrupting their conversation. He took one look at Tyson and held out a hand. "Hey, buddy."

Tyson opened his arms, and they hugged. "Jesus, I haven't seen you in forever," Tyson noted.

"Yeah, Levi called me a couple days ago. I was close by, so here I am for a visit."

"You left the navy?"

"Yeah, after I got a bit of an injury." He winced. "Figured it was probably time to take this old bod and do something different with it."

"I don't want to burst your bubble," Tyson began, "but it's not necessarily different here. Sometimes it's far more dangerous."

"I don't have any illusions," Steven noted. "Besides, no guarantee Levi even wants me at this point." He turned toward Levi at the table.

"I can't imagine he wouldn't." Tyson also eyed Levi, one eyebrow raising. "He knows good men when he sees them. Damn, he's pretty well cleaned out every group I ever worked with at this point."

Steven chuckled. "Yeah, an underground gossip channel says he's always looking for good men." He walked over to the dining room table and sat down near Levi. "So, you mentioned something about California. You know I just came from there, right?"

"I know. And you were looking to relocate here."

"That's just a thought."

Levi smirked.

"There might be a woman involved too," Steven shared.

At that, Tyson smiled. "Any reason you're avoiding California?"

"No," Steven replied, but he spoke a little too fast.

At that, Tyson just smiled. "Relationship trouble?"

"Isn't it always?" Steven asked.

"Serious?"

"No, not at all," he murmured. "So, do you want to tell

me about this job, instead of talking about my nonexistent love life?"

"Do you have a love life?" Levi asked.

"Not anymore," Steven said.

"Ah, anyone you want to resurrect things with?"

"Nope, I sure don't. I don't like cheaters."

And that went for everybody else in Levi's group too. "We all agree with you there," Levi confirmed. "So it's Northern California, near Fort Bragg actually."

"That's a small-ass town. What the hell's wrong up there?"

"Heard talk about something happening on the nearby coast," Levi mentioned.

Steven stared at him. "Okay, and what about it?"

"Apparently the tides up there are washing things in that are worrying some people."

"So that's a matter for the local cops, right? Surely it's got nothing to do with us."

"In this particular case, a woman washed up on shore—alive, but barely—and, if it weren't for some sloppy handling, she would have done better. She nearly died, and the family wants us to investigate and to find out what the hell's really going on."

"That's not exactly the kind of work I thought we'd be doing," Steven replied.

"That's what I meant by you never really know around here," Tyson stated. "Our cases span everything from a domestic kidnapping to *Hey, we'll ship you to Israel because somebody's looking for support.*"

"That's quite a span all right." Turning back to Levi, Steven asked, "So, this woman, is she okay?"

"She might be, and I think you also know her."

At that, Steven frowned and shook his head. "I sure as hell hope not," he snapped.

"Her name is Opal."

At that, he reared back. "Jesus Christ." Bolting to his feet, he seemed ready to run.

"Don't worry," Levi said. "We're flying you right back out again."

He stared and asked, "And the cops haven't gotten to the bottom of this?"

"No, apparently Opal's father has been in trouble a lot, so there is talk that this might have some undercurrents where the law is having some problems with them."

"Yeah, you could say so. He was a dirty cop. All his cases had to be reopened. Cases that the other cops had worked hard at closing, but, because of his transgressions and evidence swaps, everything he'd touched had to be audited. Opal went through a ton of shit over that, and it wasn't her fault."

"No, but you know what that's like."

"Sure I do. So are you thinking this is another cop or something?"

"We're not exactly sure what it is. I was wondering if you were willing to go on the payroll to sort out this cluster-fuck for me."

"Hell, I'll do it for free. Opal and I go way back. When do I leave?"

"Now, but you aren't going alone."

Steven glared at Levi, his gaze as hard as flint, and snapped, "I don't need anybody with me. I know the area, and I know the players involved."

"That may be," Levi hedged, "but that doesn't mean you're completely detached from the whole matter."

He stopped, then winced. "You could be right there," he admitted. He looked over at Tyson and asked, "Are you coming?"

"No. I just got back from an op."

"I'll send you over with Reyes, as he's got family close by there too," Levi replied.

"Good enough," Steven replied, "I know him too. You really did steal all the good guys, didn't you?"

"Sure did." Levi gave him a fat grin. "And I won't apologize for any of it. Check in as soon as you land. Go get your gear and meet up with Reyes."

"I'm already on the way." Steven ran out of the building to face demons that he'd buried a long time ago.

Chapter 1

S TEVEN FRANKLIN AND Reyes Drere, his partner on this job, exited the airplane at Fort Bragg Airport, California, and stepped out onto the tarmac. He looked over at Reyes. "You want to go pick up the rental vehicle?"

"Sure," Reyes replied. "I'll meet you back here in a few minutes." With that, he headed off to the left, toward the rental office.

Steven could have gone with him, except he wanted to try calling Opal again. He'd called her several times since he'd found out he was coming but had gotten absolutely no response, which worried him more than anything.

As he stood here trying again, while waiting for Reyes to come back with the car, a man approached. Much older, he looked as if he'd been hell on wheels as a younger man, and even now appeared that he could handle himself.

"You're Steven Franklin," he said briskly, as he approached. It was more of a statement than a question.

"I am." Steven studied him curiously. "Can I help you?"

"I have a message for you."

At that, Steven stiffened. "What message?" There was enough suspicion in his voice to warn off the guy, yet, at the same time, to let him know Steven was listening.

"You've been calling for somebody. She can't answer."

Who was this guy, and what did he know about Opal?

He glared at the man. "Why can't she answer?"

"All communications have been blocked."

Steven didn't like this one bit. "Who blocked the communication? Is she a prisoner? What's this got to do with you?"

"I know where she is, and I can take you to her," he murmured. "That's all I'll say out here."

Steven studied the grizzled man. "Why you?"

Another bitter smile came Steven's way. "Long story. Plus we don't have time."

"I'm not going anywhere without my partner."

"Yeah. You came with Reyes."

At that, Steven's eyebrows shot up. "What do you know about Reyes?"

"Straight shooter, comes from hard, long family relations down south. He currently works for Levi, and so do you."

"You know Levi?"

"I know *of* Levi," he muttered. "I don't have a military background. I'm local PD."

"Still?"

"No," he snapped. "Hell no."

"But that's your connection to Opal, isn't it?"

"Yes," he said grimly. "Now enough talking. You need to follow me."

"Will do, when I get the rental here."

He nodded. "At the street behind the airport, look for an old beat-up Ford pickup. It would have been black in the day, but it's more of a charcoal gray now and dirty as hell." With that, he turned and walked away.

Reyes drove up a moment later, in a white SUV, as Steven managed to quickly snap an image of the older guy with his phone, while he had the chance. Steven pointed at the retreating man and asked Reyes, "Do you know him?"

"No, I don't." He shook his head. "What's going on?"

"He approached me and told me to follow him, if we want to hook up with Opal."

At that, Reyes frowned at him. "Do we trust him?"

"Hell no, but I don't think he trusts us either."

"Interesting. Has she gone into hiding?" Reyes asked.

Steven nodded. "Which isn't a bad idea and would explain why we can't reach her by phone."

"Yet somebody's monitoring her phone, otherwise how did he know you were here? Did you text her?"

He nodded. "I texted her and told her that I was coming in on this flight."

"That answers that. Let's go."

Driving the rental SUV, Reyes followed the retired cop's instructions to get off the airport grounds and onto the main street. As they came up to the final turn to get to the back of the area, a beat-up faded-black Ford pickup, dusty as hell, pulled out in front of them.

"That's him," Steven said.

"Good. He certainly seems to know his way around. He's a local cop, you say?"

"Yeah, but retired, I think—or canned, for all I know."

"Right, given the family situation, it could be either."

"It was a pretty bad scenario here with her father. A dirty cop who ended up tainting a lot of good cases. Caused a lot of trouble. He made a lot of enemies, and anybody involved with him got painted with the same brush."

"Right, it's never fun when that happens. The question is, do we trust him?"

"I don't trust anybody," Steven snapped. "Yet Opal is a hell of a good person, and I don't want to see her hurt any more than she already has been. If she is in hiding, obviously they think her life is still in danger."

"Sounds like it," Reyes murmured. "Let's follow this guy and see what happens." The old truck led them on a merry dance, but he kept the GPS running on his phone to track their travels. "Interesting route."

"Not exactly convoluted though," Steven noted, "as we're heading right out of town."

"And that goes along with what we know, right?"

"Her family lives out here, so maybe she's been staying at her mother's place—which isn't some great hiding place, as that would be obvious as hell to the bad guys."

"We still don't understand what all went on, but it sounded pretty rough."

"From what Levi could gather, it was. But details are sketchy, and those came from the family. Still, Levi thought they were reluctant to say too much on the phone."

"Afraid that their phones were being tracked?"

"Maybe," he murmured. After another ten minutes of following this guy, they realized he was really taking them on a circuitous route.

"So, is he trying to keep us, lose us, or lose somebody else?" Reyes asked.

"Who knows," Steven replied. "We seem to be heading to her mom's place. If so, all this circling around doesn't matter. The bad guys already know where her mother lives. Still, this old guy is the best lead we've got right now, and I need to connect with Opal somehow to find out what the hell's going on."

"Agreed, I've got no problem doing this, but it's interesting that he was there waiting for us."

"I think we can put that down to Opal's family."

"Maybe, but we could have used a little better intel and instructions, unless they just aren't sure who to trust or aren't confident in using their phones."

"Yeah, the phone thing makes sense to a certain point," Steven murmured, pulling up the GPS tracking their route, "particularly if they think—" He stopped, looked over at Reyes. "Do they think it has anything to do with local law officials, who may have access to their telephone calls?"

"Hell, even if they don't have access, nearly anything can be bought these days. So much for search warrants and the necessities for all that stuff, *huh*?" Reyes noted.

"Right. How's your family, by the way?"

"They're great." He grinned. "I'm hoping to spend a few days with them after this case is over."

"Good to know," he murmured. "Levi doesn't mind things like that?"

"No, not at all. It doesn't matter to him, and we can head home whenever we need to. As long as we're not completely overwhelmed with work, that is. I get to stop and visit pretty frequently, which is better than most jobs," Reyes added. "Some families need healing, and, in our case, we need a lot of it, so I'm working on it."

"At least you're working on it. An awful lot of guys can't be bothered."

"Yep."

"If you don't mind me asking, are you married?"

"I am," Reyes declared. "We had a small private ceremony, just the two of us. She's been to hell and back with her family, and honestly, I can't say that mine was any easier, so it was complicated to even bring our families in on our plans. We finally decided to avoid that whole scenario and got married on our own."

"Hey, I can't blame you there," Steven murmured. "After making all the plans for a big wedding on my end, only to have it all blow up in my face right before it all, you can bet I'll never have a big one, and I'm not so sure I'd have a wedding at all."

"Sorry. That's a tough deal."

"It is what it is." Steven shrugged. "And for the best really. Much better to find out she's cheating sooner than later, you know?"

"Definitely, but it still sucks."

"It really does, and it makes you look twice at the men around you too."

"Yeah, that's awful and definitely not the way you want to go through life," Reyes admitted. "Hope you are not talking about Opal here."

"No way. Opal and I go way back, strictly as friends. Plus Opal's no cheater."

Finally the retired cop in the old truck in front of them pulled into a driveway, leading to a large house surrounded by big trees. He drove right into the garage.

The large gate, open at the moment, gave Reyes and Steven access to drive forward too.

"Interesting that he's going right into the garage. I guess that leaves us out front."

"Possibly able to leave quickly … but maybe not." With the gate shutting behind them, they were not leaving anytime soon.

"This is not Opal's family home, but we are somewhere nearby. So not sure who this belongs to."

"Text the address to Levi. He'll get any information available."

"Will do. The gate must open automatically when we're

ready to leave, but, for now, I'm not leaving until we get some answers. I want to know where the hell Opal is and if she's okay."

"You really care about her, don't you?"

"I do. I even thought about marrying her."

"Whoa."

Steven laughed. "Easy, tiger. She wasn't ready, I wasn't ready, and it would have been a stupid move. Yet I did think about it afterward and wonder."

"Oh, I hear you, and I think Levi may be a little too smart for his own good."

"What do you mean?" Steven asked.

"Oh, nothing," Reyes murmured, with a grin. "You'll see."

Steven shook his head at that. "You guys are really into the cryptic clues, aren't you?"

"Not really, but apparently Levi's caught the bug from Ice." Reyes pulled the SUV beyond the front door and parked. "You ready for this?" Reyes asked Steven.

"Hell, yes, I've been trying to reach Opal since I found out she was in trouble." At that, he hopped out of the SUV and walked up to the front door, with Reyes at his side. The door opened before he reached it, but nobody was there. He stepped inside. "Opal, where are you?"

When no answer came, he called out. "Damn it, Opal. Answer me." The sounds of a woman crying—as she tried to speak, with more tears than vocal cords—had Steven turning. Opal stood there, her hands on her cheeks, staring at him in wordless wonder, tears streaming down her face.

She looked like she had recently been in the boxing ring—and had clearly lost. And his heart hurt at the pain she must have endured.

He raced over and was about to grab her and to scoop her up, when another woman snapped, "Easy. Be careful. She's hurt."

That stopped him midstride. His arms came around her in a gentle hug that touched her less and became more of a caress than anything. Her arms closed around his neck, and she dropped her forehead against his chest, almost as if a benediction.

He whispered against her ear, "Jesus, what happened?"

She took a step back. "I can't talk much," she whispered, her voice both raw and hoarse. "And definitely not on the phone."

And that made sense in a way that he couldn't understand before. She led him into another room, where they were shown to the couch. He turned to look at her mother, standing behind a big writing desk, and the grizzled old man that led them here now stood beside her. Steven walked over and shook hands with her mother. "I don't know if you remember me," Steven began. "It's been quite a few years."

She gave them the briefest of smiles. "I do remember you," she replied, "from a much easier time."

He nodded. "I'm sorry for all the trouble you've had these last few years."

"Thank you. Sometimes you don't know what life has in store for you. You think you know what's going on, and then you find out you don't know anything at all." Her tone was harsh, as if condemning herself and the rest of the world.

Not a whole lot Steven could say to that, so he walked back over to Opal, who sat on the couch, a slow trickle of tears moving down her cheeks.

He bent down in front of her and gently held her in his arms, while he was on his knees. Her head rested against his shoulder, and he felt her frame shaking. "My God," he whispered. "You have to tell me who did this. I'll take care of it."

She pulled back, a wistful smile on her face, her hand gently stroking his cheek. "Always the avenging angel," she murmured, her voice raspy and harsh.

He gently touched her throat, seeing the marks on her neck. "They tried to strangle you?"

She nodded.

"Damaged vocal cords from that, I presume?"

She nodded again.

"Will they heal?"

She nodded in the affirmative once more.

"That's a good thing. Maybe I won't make them suffer quite as long."

Again a smile broke over her face, and she ever-so-gently gave him a kiss on the cheek. He closed his eyes, the two of them cheek to cheek, as he whispered, "I'd have done anything to not have this happen to you."

And yet again she nodded. "I'm so happy you're here."

"I would have been here earlier," he snapped, glaring at her, "if you had told me."

She pointed to her throat. "Haven't been out of hospital long."

He nodded. "So you did go to the hospital?"

She nodded again.

At that, he looked over at the grizzled old man. "Any chance you were able to wipe the records?"

He gave a knowing smirk. "Let's just say that somebody at the medical center changed the file number and the name."

Steven straightened. "Now I need to hear what you guys

15

know, and why the hell we're being so clandestine?"

At that, the mother spoke up. "It's a long story."

"They're all about long stories, but it usually boils down to very simple things."

She frowned at him. "What do you mean?"

"Revenge, greed, power, or love. Not a whole lot else really comes into play with something like this," he said simply. "Sex to a certain extent, but that's usually part of revenge and power."

Opal's mother sighed. "It seems odd to boil down our entire lives to that."

"True," Reyes noted, trying to soften the rough edges a bit, "but what Steven is saying is that it's important to identify what's at the heart of it."

"Oh, sorry, this is Reyes, my partner," Steven added. "He's from south of here, and he's worked for Levi for a long time."

Opal's mother nodded a little more formally. "It's nice to meet you."

He smiled gently. "Nice to meet you too, ma'am."

But the grizzled guy frowned at him. "Your family owns that huge landscaping greenery company, don't they?"

Reyes nodded. "Yeah, and, if you know that, I'm sure you've heard all about the trouble that happened a few years back."

"I did. Murder, suicide, a mess, right?" He hooked his thumbs in his belt loops and studied Reyes.

"Yeah, they're all kind of a mess," he said calmly. "The only good thing is, when a deal like that is over, it's over."

"I would like to think that this could be over as well," Opal's mother noted, looking at him. "Please call me Ruby."

Reyes smiled and asked, "Any other children? Or is Opal

an only child?"

"No, we had always hoped for more, but it never happened."

Reyes noted, "Maybe right now that's a good thing. We only have one to keep safe."

"It's not just keeping her safe. It's also about getting to the bottom of this, so she doesn't have to look over her shoulders for the rest of her life," her mother said, her voice quivering.

"So, this was very targeted then. Do you feel it's related to what happened to your husband?"

"We don't know yet, but that's a possibility."

"Who rescued her?" Steven asked.

Ruby hesitated and then motioned at the grizzled man. "This is Marshal. He saw the kidnapping, as it happened, but couldn't break into the warehouse in time to save her, while they were working her over. Still, he followed them down to the marina, where they put her on a boat and took her out. It was a good thing he saw it, and he immediately grabbed light scuba gear, then went out in a boat himself and followed at a safe distance.

"When they pulled up and stopped, he pulled up for a moment, quickly geared up a short distance away, then headed toward it. They had put cement blocks on her shoes, tied them with ropes around her throat, and threw her overboard, alive." Tears slowly ran down her face.

Nearly beside himself, Steven was speechless. "That's … God, I don't even know what to say. Go on."

"She was semiconscious from the beating they'd given her, and, by the time Marshal reached her, which wasn't very long when you think about it, she was nearly gone. He immediately shared his oxygen while he cut her ropes and got her back to his boat, somehow keeping her alive. But it was days later before she regained consciousness."

At that, Steven looked over at the grizzled man with respect. "That's pretty good timing."

"It was," he agreed, "and you can accuse me all you want, but, no, I didn't know what the hell they were doing with her. Maybe I should have called the cops, but a part of me was afraid it *was* the cops."

At that, Reyes stiffened and looked over at him. "Was it revenge then?"

"We don't know," Marshal admitted. "I don't have any good images of the guys either. As much as I had hoped the pictures I took would turn out halfway clear, they didn't. The photos are smudges. Nothing's identifiable, and honestly, it's a shitstorm from beginning to end."

"Were a lot of other boats around?"

He nodded. "There were, to a certain extent, but I wasn't alone on my boat, if that's what you're really asking. For the moment, I need to keep my partner's identity hidden, as much as I can. He was there in the moment, and I called on him for help, and he agreed to get me out to Opal, and he had the gear. He is the one who helped me pull her in from the water." He shrugged. "More important, he's a doctor, so that helped."

"Yeah, you're not kidding. Was he out fishing?"

"He was." Marshal stared at Steven. "What made you think of that?"

"I've known a couple doctors. It's a demanding field, and they tend to hit the water, as a way to change their environment and to dissolve the stress."

"That's definitely what he was doing, and I happened to know him. When I explained what was going on, he didn't waste any time. He's the one who saw them throw her overboard. I was already in the water, heading toward them."

"Got it, so that's how the timing worked out so well." Even at that explanation, the timing was incredible. She'd been a heartbeat from death. Steven turned to face her, his gaze dropping to the mark on her neck, hating that she got caught up in something way over her head, something not of her own doing. He turned back to Marshal.

Marshal continued. "Exactly, I was afraid they would do something like that. I just, ... in my heart of hearts, I knew. Still, I couldn't believe they would do that. Yet they did it without any hesitation, according to the doc."

"I'll need to talk to him."

Marshal frowned at that.

"Just talk. I have no intention of grilling him or anything else, but he might have seen something that you didn't ask him about."

"He might have, so, for her sake, I'll ask him. That's all I'm prepared to do."

"Got it, but now that we're on this," Steven declared, trying to make it not sound too rude, "no way I'll leave any stone unturned."

Marshal glared at him openly, and Steven realized that his tone was not interpreted correctly, so he added, "Remember. It's not a vigilante quest here. She needs her life back."

"Oh, I get it," Marshal snapped. "That is my whole goal. That she gets a life, a real one."

Steven looked over at Opal and smiled gently. "I'll do anything I can."

Her own gaze was teary-eyed, as she nodded. "I know you will. That's who you are."

"It is, but a lot more is going on with this thing, and we need to hear everything."

"The only other thing to add," Marshal stated, "outside of pulling in the case files, depends on whether you know about what the family has gone through."

Steven cocked his head. "Her father was a cop, a dirty cop, and all his cases were reopened. Especially after he confessed, those cases were all audited. So a lot of hard policework went down the tube because of him."

Marshal nodded. "Exactly, not only are there cops who hate Roscoe's guts for what he did but an awful lot of criminals were released, who also hated Roscoe in the first place, and now are back out in the world. Too many people out there want to silence him, in case he talks any more. Then we have all the victims and their families in all those overturned cases who were definitely not happy when the perpetrators were released."

Steven noted how Reyes had leaned against the wall, choosing a position that offered his partner a great view of all involved here. Steven appreciated Reyes's forethought. Steven trusted Opal implicitly; her mother, Ruby, only slightly; and didn't know or trust Marshal at all.

"So, in other words, we're not short on suspects." Reyes voiced what they all were thinking.

"So I should also state the obvious." Marshal hesitated and then added, "I guess you don't know, or at least I assume you don't know the latest."

"No, I probably don't." Steven stared at him, frowning. "What's the latest?"

"My father is dead," Opal whispered. "He died in jail, the same day I was kidnapped and nearly murdered."

"How?"

"They say it was a suicide," Ruby said from Marshal's side.

As in very close to Marshal's side, letting everyone know about their relationship.

"They? They who? Was he on suicide watch?"

"The prison. And, no, he was not on suicide watch," Ruby replied. "I'm not supposed to be happy about it, but he's caused us so much grief that it's hard to be upset and to feel the loss. After everything that had happened, I just ... his death felt imminent in a way. I'm grieving the loss of the life that we had together, but it's hard for me to grieve for him personally."

"Understood," Steven said cautiously. "Of course, not knowing whether it was suicide or not makes a difference."

"It does, and yet it doesn't, at least for me," Ruby admitted. "He's dead. I don't even know how to feel about whether he was murdered or not." Ruby glared at Steven. "I'm not sure I care. Lots of people had a stake in this, and these overturned cases bring up way-too-many people."

"So why did anyone go after your daughter?" Steven asked. "Opal had nothing to do with Roscoe's cases or his actions."

"I don't know," Ruby said, once again bringing her hand to her mouth. She shook her head, as if it was too much for her to even think about.

And maybe it was. She'd been to hell and back over her husband and then again over her daughter's kidnapping and near-death event.

Steven looked back at Opal. "Did you have anything to do with his cases?" She shook her head. "How about his cohorts?"

"Only Marshal," she whispered.

21

Steven turned and addressed Marshal. "What was your role in Roscoe's life?"

"Best friend and partners in the force," he said succinctly, "but I had no idea he was dirty. I went to bat for him, sick to my gut, trying to tell everybody they were wrong, and then he confessed." He glared at Steven. "That's when my whole world blew apart too."

"Ouch," Reyes muttered under his breath. "Now that would suck."

"It does. It's a betrayal at the deepest level because we weren't just best friends, we were partners. I had to leave the force because I couldn't handle all the looks, all the suspicions, the steady stream of interrogations because I was on so many cases with him. I had no idea what he was doing, but nobody would believe me."

"No, they wouldn't." Reyes nodded. "You were guilty by association. I can understand the sentiment. For the rest of your life you would always be judged by your partner's actions."

"Exactly, and being judged because of your partner isn't a problem when your partner is a decent man." Marshal shook his head and stared off in the distance. "However, being judged when your partner is a lying piece of shit, that's a problem."

That also explained, to a certain extent, why Marshal was helping the family.

The proximity between Marshal and Ruby explained a lot too. Their loss was almost the same. They had both been betrayed by and had lost their trusted partner.

OPAL OPENED HER eyes once again, noting Steven was still

here beside her, still watching her, even when she slept. She'd curled up in a corner of the sofa in exhaustion, shaken to the core, dealing with withdrawals from the drugs the doctor had given her, plus the shock and trauma of what she'd been through, then finding out her father was dead. Yet some of that shaking was about seeing Steven again.

Even now she touched his massive forearm, feeling the instant warmth and all that inherent strength. He quickly engulfed her in the gentlest of hugs. He'd always been a big teddy bear and a very special part of her life. Sure, time had made a lot of changes in their relationship, but, at the core, he was still a special part of her life. And honestly, while she'd been tortured and dying, all she could do was wonder why he wasn't coming to save her.

Of course he had no way of knowing what was going on and no way of finding out at the time. But, even as she was held captive, she had hoped that her mother had contacted Steven. Yet there was no reason for it. He was in the navy— or so she had thought. Somehow Marshal had found Levi's group which had been the connection to Steven. ... That Steven was here now was nothing short of a miracle.

Trying to get a hold of him, while everybody else was busily trying to keep her away from all communication with anybody, was also a different story. That he was here now just broke her heart and yet filled the empty voids in her life.

He looked over at her, his hand in hers, and whispered, "Wouldn't you be more comfortable if you were in bed?"

She shook her head. "I don't sleep well."

He gave her an understanding smile. "I'm sure you don't. Sometimes life really is the thing of nightmares."

Opal knew Steven would understand, but still, what she hated was her constant weepiness that seemed to come so easily. She wasn't normally so quick to tears. "I think I've lost my job," she murmured.

He stared at her. "What were you doing?"

"Trying to complete my degree."

"Ah, well, I'm not sure that you can get a special dispensation for that, can you?"

"Not really classes. I was doing a practicum," she murmured, closing her eyes when it was hard to swallow. Immediately her glass of water was held to her lips, she smiled, took a sip, and managed to swallow. "Thank you."

"Do they know what happened?" Steven asked Opal, then turned to Ruby, hoping to save Opal further strain on her damaged vocal cords.

Ruby nodded. "I contacted them personally, told them how Opal had been hospitalized and was very ill. ... I had to tell them that she was home and that we weren't sure yet what the future would hold in terms of her recovery. I also told them that I would let them know about her returning as soon as possible."

"Right, so that left them in a bit of a bind, but that's absolutely nothing compared to what you've been through," Steven said to Opal. "So any understanding person would have no problem with you going back, when this is over."

"Will this ever be over?" Opal asked, voicing one of the fears she hadn't been able to get out of her mind. "I'm not handling it well. I don't sleep. I can't even close my eyes half the time for the images and the fear waiting for me."

He nodded immediately. "It will be there for a while. I can't tell you if it'll be over today or tomorrow. I won't lie to you because sometimes this shit takes time. However, we'll make sure that you're safe at all times."

"And yet I don't want to live as a prisoner."

"Of course not," he murmured. "But you won't live at all if we don't handle this right," he said, making it quite clear what the choices could be.

She groaned. "I get it. I do. And I've never felt that as much as I did when I was a prisoner."

"What did they want?" Reyes asked. "Can you tell us some of their questions?"

"They were looking for a stash."

"Ah, did your father end up with a hoard of money that he maybe didn't give back?" Steven asked, looking over at Ruby.

Ruby shook her head. "If he did, I don't know anything about it, and I've never seen any big money or bank accounts that had big money."

"Right, and do we know it's money?" Steven asked. "I hate to say it, but what are the chances it could have been drugs?"

At that, Ruby's face paled. "I don't know," she whispered. "I gave Marshal the run of the house to try and figure out anything and everything he could, but I don't think he found anything." She looked over at Marshal.

He shook his head. "Nothing I could find. When they picked up Opal, I wondered why her and not Ruby because, in theory, Ruby would have potentially been a better avenue for information. I think the bottom line is that they're guessing, hoping that Opal might know something. Also ... the fact that they're looking for a stash made me think that it may not be law enforcement involved, but I can't guarantee that. If anybody thought her father had a big bankroll set aside for better days, then it's quite possible they thought they could take the money and run."

Part of the problem for Opal was that, every time she

closed her eyes, the same scenario kept hammering at her, over and over again. She was scared to sleep, terrified that, when she woke up, she would still be caught in the nightmare she'd escaped from.

Honestly, she hadn't escaped. Marshal had rescued her—and in the nick of time. That was something she would be forever grateful for. Opal had been hesitant early on, as she had watched the relationship developing between her mother and Marshal. Opal understood her mother's need to have somebody stand at her side and to believe in her, and the two of them had both been crushed by her father's actions.

Yet now they all had to deal with the grief and the pain of Roscoe's loss. Because he was an asshole didn't change all the time he'd been such a big part of their lives. And even now that he'd turned out to be something different than Opal had hoped her father was, it didn't diminish the reality that she had to deal with a very confusing mess of emotions now that he was gone. None of this was easy.

She yawned and closed her eyes ever-so-slightly.

"Rest," Steven said, his big hand gently covering hers, "unless you want to go to bed."

She immediately shook her head. "No, no, I can't go to bed." She heard the panic in her own voice, but it was beyond her control. He immediately squeezed her fingers, then shifted his position, so she now rested at his side. Instead of her head against the arm of the couch, she leaned against him.

"Now," he whispered, "go to sleep. Nobody will get you for the next little bit. I'm here, and I won't leave. I promise."

She stared up at him, realizing he'd instantly understood the fear inside her. She swallowed hard, and then, assessing how she felt, she nodded. "Maybe I'll try. Thank you for that."

"Anytime, sweetheart, anytime."

And, with that, she closed her eyes, snuggled closer, and drifted off to sleep.

Chapter 2

OPAL WOKE WITH a sudden panic. Almost instantly, warm hands reached out to soothe and to hold her, not tight, but in a light grasp, and she heard a voice coming through the blackness in her mind.

"It's all right. You're safe," Steven murmured. "I have you."

She collapsed against him, not wanting the tears to pour like they always did, but knowing there wasn't any way to stop them.

He didn't say anything and just held her.

When the tears finally dried up, she faced him. "As you can tell, healing is not happening."

He gave her a lopsided grin. "Healing *is* happening. The tears are part of it."

She wiped her eyes and looked over to realize that everybody was still in the living room. She winced. "Nothing like making a fool of myself."

At that, Reyes gave her a headshake. "Don't ever think that. Healing has to happen in its own way, in its own shape, and in its own time. You can't rush it. I tried, and it doesn't work."

She stared at him and realized that he must have his own demons too. She nodded slowly. "Thank you for that. If I fall asleep, I wake up in agony and usually in an outright panic," she murmured. She brushed the hair from her face, and then noted with surprise that she *was* feeling better. Decent, in fact. "I don't think I've slept that well in days." She looked up at Steven. "Thanks for lending me your shoulder."

"You're welcome to my shoulder anytime." He smiled calmly. "Knowing that you're safe allows your subconscious and your defenses to drop down, so you can really relax. You need that just like everybody else does. Don't block it. Sleep is the most valuable thing you can get for yourself right now, in order to heal, and you need to get it anytime there's an opportunity."

She smiled. "You make it sound as if it's something I can reach out and grab."

"If it isn't, then anytime the opportunity presents itself, grab it. You don't ever have to apologize to the rest of us."

Opal smiled, as she looked over at her mother, who was nodding.

"You did sleep," Ruby confirmed, "not for very long, but it's the deepest sleep I've seen you get in a while."

Opal laughed. "There's something very indestructible about Steven. I guess, for a moment, I realized it was safe enough to let down my guard and to relax a little."

"Good," Ruby said, with tears in her eyes. She turned to Marshal. "I've been very grateful for Marshal's help these last few days. Ever since my husband died, the media intrusion in our lives has been even worse. The phone is ringing off the hook, with reporters, journalists, and everybody else trying to get another piece of us. We went through hell when he was convicted, and then, when he started confessing, it was even worse," she murmured. "I'm struggling to stay afloat myself."

"Have you made funeral arrangements?" Reyes asked.

She sighed. "It's not something we had planned for before it happened, and I certainly didn't plan for him to be in jail at the time of his death. So I guess my answer would be *somewhat*." Then she gave a broken laugh and added, "And that's only because of the effort Marshal's done on that. The body has been released to a funeral home. I think a simple unceremonious cremation might be the best thing at this point."

"I think so too," Reyes agreed. "You don't want a big funeral procession, I presume."

"God, no." She shuddered. "There was still a part of him that was a good man. I just don't know what happened to make him do what he did. It's really hard to walk away from all the years we had together as a happily married couple. However, once you understand how different the person you married had become, it changes everything. I want this to go away, and I want it to go away in a nice, quiet, and yet respectful manner. Some of the public remarks have been … horrid."

"Can you give us details?

Ruby shuddered again. "They're really gruesome. They want his body tarred and feathered, his head on a pike for all to see. It's anything and everything. Somebody from the prison posted that he was gone, causing the news media interest to explode, and the comments were so horrible that we had to turn them off. They were foul."

"That's people for you," Steven murmured, his arm sliding around Opal, shifting her up against him.

"Indeed," Ruby agreed, "but it doesn't make it any easier for those of us who have nowhere to go to get away from it."

"No, of course not," he murmured. "Just keep holding on. Once Roscoe is buried, all of this will die down."

"I hope so, but, if not, it means my daughter is still in danger."

Opal stood up slowly and walked stiffly. "Mom, no need to panic. We will cross that bridge when we get to it. I'll be right back." She used the facilities and then washed her face, trying to put some of her sense of self back together again. She did feel pleasantly alive for the first time in a very long time. The fear was still there, yet, for the first time, it was muted in the background.

She didn't know how much of that was the sleep versus having Steven here to help out. No doubt she felt stronger with him around, but then he had always had the ability to make her feel as if she counted. He made her feel alive, special even. She didn't even know if he could do anything with this mess, but, if he could, she knew he would do his best.

She was blessed to have him and was also sad that they had lost touch over the years. She didn't really know why, but they had drifted apart. He'd always been busy on missions and not able to tell her very much about them. She'd heard through the grapevine at some point that he was engaged. It had saddened her for her own sake, and somehow she still knew his fiancée was a very lucky woman.

He hadn't mentioned it to her, but then why would he? So far it had been all about Opal and what had happened with her dad. It's not that she wanted to steer the conversation to Steven's engagement, but it was hard not to, when there was so much mess in Opal's world. Any other subject would be easier to talk about.

When she made her way back to rejoin them, Opal looked over at her mother and asked, "Are there leftovers or anything?"

"Oh my." Her mother stared at Opal in amazement. "Are you hungry?"

She nodded. "I think I am, yes," she murmured, "though I'm not sure how that happened."

"I don't care how it happened, but I'll go get you something, something easy for your throat." She stopped and looked from Steven to Reyes and asked, "Have you guys eaten?"

They shared a glance and a shrug. Steven shook his head. "We can catch something later, and we still have to check into our hotel."

At hearing that, the word instantly exploded from Opal's mouth. "No!"

"What does that mean?" Steven asked Opal gently.

She took a deep breath. "Please stay here," she whispered, the slightest waver in her voice. That said so much, even as she tried to stop it from showing.

He looked at her for a long moment and then nodded. "I guess we can stay for a while, yes."

"It'll reduce our movements back and forth, so we wouldn't be followed quite so easily," Reyes added.

Steven interrupted, "But you also know it's temporary, right, Opal?"

She gave him a ghost of a smile. "Of course, but maybe in the meantime I can regain some strength and self-confidence and grab some sleep. Having you two around is a huge boon for that."

"I get that," Steven murmured, then looked over at Reyes. "What do you think? Do you see any problem with that?"

Reyes shook his head. "Nope, if there is room for us, it would be perfect. We'll need a table or desk to work at too."

"We have lots of that," Opal shared. "This rental house has plenty of spare rooms. Even though we didn't move very far, we left home to get away from the media. I'm pretty sure Mom is bound to be looking at selling that house, now that my father is gone."

Steven nodded. "That may not a bad idea, as the place is full of memories, I'm sure. What about you? Were you still living there?"

"No, I have an apartment, but we gave notice, although I still need to get everything moved out," she said, with a wince. "I only have a couple weeks left, and I'm definitely not looking forward to that." She brushed back her hair and added, "I can't seem to think that far ahead."

"Hire it out. Move whatever is there into a storage unit for now. You don't know where you might end up living," Steven suggested instantly. "Then you don't need anybody to know what happened. You don't need to see anyone. You just need it taken care of. That's why you hire people."

She stared at him and then nodded. "You may be right. I *was* avoiding dealing with it. I could have just paid another four months' worth of rent, but the media found my apartment."

"Sounds like a good reason to me. I can help now that I am here."

"It's been a long time to reach out. I'm sorry for that," she muttered.

"Don't be sorry. You're not to blame. It was just life."

"I was thinking about that, when I came out of the bathroom just now, wondering how we let so many years get between us."

"It doesn't matter now because we've reconnected again, and I'll always be there for you. Whenever you need me, I'm there."

"I do know that," she murmured. "My mother wasn't so sure that you were coming, but I'm grateful that Levi went the extra mile to make it happen."

"And how do you know Levi?"

Opal glanced at her mother and explained, "Ice's father has a medical facility here."

Steven sat back, nodding. "Of course. I'd forgotten that. And that's how your hospitalization records were changed, I presume?" Steven shot a look at Marshal, then to Opal.

"Yeah, it sure is," Opal confirmed.

"If it helps," Ruby added, "the records will be corrected later, but, for the moment, to keep her identity hidden and to keep her safe, Dr. Danning was happy to do whatever needed to be done."

Reyes noted, "Plus your kidnappers and would-be killers may not yet know that you survived this, Opal. So best to keep you hidden, especially as we delve into this more."

Then Steven spoke up. "So, that led to Ice, which led to me. And you're really lucky because I had only contacted Levi recently about joining his team. He's always had an open-door policy for anybody looking for work," Steven explained. "We all come out of whatever military service area we served in, and a lot of us have gone to work for Levi. It's crazy how many former military guys Levi has brought on. Baffling almost that you could locate me so quickly." He stared at Opal. "Actually it's a miracle."

Ruby added, "But it's good that you all come with abilities that most people don't have access to."

"Exactly," Steven agreed, "and, in this case, Levi and Ice have access to a ton of civilian experts too, including medical staff and facilities apparently."

Opal smiled. "The hospital staff put in a lot of work to keep me alive. I don't think it was easy. My lungs had water in them. My throat was damaged. I'd taken quite a few blows to the face, and, although not all my bones were broken, several were, and it's taken a while to heal. Even now, my face might need plastic surgery, when the swelling goes down."

Steven held her face, while he critically assessed the damage, then shrugged. "You still look beautiful to me."

She gave him a dry look. "I almost believe you. I know when you look at my face that you don't see my face. You were always more concerned about the me on the inside."

"When I first saw your face, and there was nobody I could punch to take out my aggravation on," he murmured, "there wasn't a whole lot of sense in focusing on it. However, you can bet that I didn't miss the damage done."

"No, of course not," she murmured. "How could you? It's pretty obvious."

"Oh, it's not that bad," Steven told her. "It's really not that bad."

"Oh please," she cried out in a hoarse voice.

"Okay, it's terrible." He chuckled. "Only because you're still vain."

"I'm not still vain," she stated trying for outrage but sounding like a hoarse frog instead.

At that, Reyes broke them up with his laughing. "I'm really glad to hear that you're not vain and that you do know him as well as you do because that will help you when we start probing into your life and that of your father's," Reyes forewarned Opal. "There will be times when you want to order us out of here, and yet we can't go. Once we commit to this, we commit fully, and there's no going back."

She took a deep breath. "I understand, but there's no life for me after this if we don't solve it. They'll come for me again. Thankfully they don't even know I'm alive—at least I hope they don't."

"Have you had any interaction with the media yet?" Steven turned to look at Marshal.

Marshal stood with his arms akimbo, as he stared at him, hardly moving. "No, we've managed to keep her rescue quiet."

"So, the kidnappers are probably looking for some notice that she's missing."

"Maybe, maybe not. Her mother was supposed to be leaving for a holiday, until I contacted Ruby—once we found out what was going on."

"You mean, when you brought Opal up to the surface?"

He nodded. "More or less, yes. I'd been talking to Ruby anyway. I was supposed to join her on this vacation. You might as well know that we're in a relationship."

"Got it," Steven noted calmly, "I had a pretty good idea on that already."

He flushed. "I've known them all my life, and Opal is like a daughter to me. When I saw what was going on, I—" Then the emotions choked him. He spun away. "I'll go help Ruby with the food." And, with that, he disappeared.

Steven looked down at Opal. "Are you okay with their relationship?"

She smiled and nodded. "Yes. Marshal makes Mom happy."

THEY HAD LARGE club sandwiches and homemade soup, and Steven ate his with his usual gusto, while Opal spooned up toast soaked in her soup. As soon as they finished eating, Steven and Reyes were shown two bedrooms and a third, where they could set up their office—or they could work at the big writing desk in the living room. Steven smiled at Opal. "This is a huge house."

"Yeah." She nodded. "It was available and private."

"Which makes it perfect." Steven pointed at the upholstered armchair for Opal to have a seat. The guys sat in the wooden chairs placed before the desk.

"We moved several times over the recent years. Always bigger and fancier." She shrugged. "I wasn't privy to their finances, so the moves didn't make me question anything. I just thought they must be doing well."

"Your mother was okay with it?"

"I guess. It was important to my father, so whatever was important to him was important to her."

He nodded. "Is that part of the money stash maybe? Do you think that went to pay for it?"

"I don't know," she said sadly. "It's one of those things that we try not to look at too closely. I do expect that, as soon as this is over, the two of them will sell their own houses and move to another town. Maybe another state, I don't know."

"No reason for them to stay here, and, after this, I'm sure there's more pain than anything else."

"I get that, and a part of me understands, and another part would be sad to see my home sold, the last place where the three of us lived together, before everything went sour."

"It's already gone in theory, with just your memories left behind," Steven suggested, "and, from the sounds of your last couple years, much less these recent events, it left quite a while ago."

She stared at him and then nodded. "You were always good at putting things in perspective."

He smiled.

"Remember that later," Reyes shared. "We'll be on your case for information pretty heavily."

"I don't even know how much I can tell you."

Reyes stood to pull a recorder from his pocket and put it down on the desk beside them, before retaking his seat. "You can start with telling us how you were kidnapped."

Chapter 3

O PAL SWALLOWED HARD, then reaching for Steven's hand, she tried to gather her thoughts. "I was walking home from work. I work and live a few blocks apart," she murmured. "I was only a block away from my apartment when a vehicle pulled up beside me, and I was snatched, quite literally, right off the sidewalk."

"Did you scream?"

"I tried, but I didn't get much chance, as a hood was thrown over my head, and I felt a needle puncture in my arm." She looked down at her arm, rubbing it self-consciously. "I fought, but there were two of them. I was lifted and thrown into a vehicle. I blacked out soon afterward."

"So, they grabbed you off the street, drugged you, and took you where?"

"They took me to a warehouse, but I don't know where it was located."

"Of course." Reyes nodded. "I'm sure they went to great lengths to hide their tracks."

"Maybe, but Marshal did find me, yet too late to stave off the beatings."

Steven spoke then. "One hard question. Were you raped?"

He managed to ask the question in a calm voice, but she

heard the tightly woven thread of anger running through it. "I don't think so," she whispered. "I think they only had me for a few hours, then decided to dump me. According to the doctors, there wasn't any evidence of a sexual assault."

"In other words, you don't remember." His gaze searched hers with an intensity that pinned her in place.

"No. I don't. There was nothing in the medical findings of that sort, and honestly, I think I went unconscious pretty quickly. They weren't very easy with their fists."

"No, they wouldn't have been," he murmured. "Assholes."

She smiled, as she reached up gently and touched his face. "Maybe assholes but, in this case, maybe it's a good thing because the time they spent doing this kept me alive long enough so Marshal could save me."

Steven nodded at that. "Do you have any idea how close that rescue was?"

"I do. It's part of what keeps me awake at night."

"The *what ifs*?"

"Yeah," she murmured. "The *what ifs*. What if Marshal had waited longer? What if the boat and dive gear hadn't been right there? Obviously I wouldn't have made it, and yet, at the same time, I would be dead, and it would be over. Then it would be a case of *what ifs* for my mother. Although horrified and in agony, she would have eventually moved on, and Marshal would have helped her."

"Right, so the next question ..." Steven stopped, as he thought about it. "What time of day was it?"

"It was four-fifteen p.m.," she said promptly. "I was literally walking home after work. I had plans for the evening with a girlfriend. When she phoned my mother looking for me, they told her that I had changed my mind, as I wasn't feeling well. Since then, the story my friends and employer were told was that I was hit by a car and am away at a special rehab center, with no visitors allowed at this time. We're hoping that will hold everybody off for a little while."

"Depending on what kind of friends they are, it might not hold very long at all."

"I would have said they were good friends, but you don't really know until you get into trouble, and then you see how they react."

"How do you feel about possibly losing all of them?"

"I feel as if I already have," she murmured. "Everything feels *over*. What happened to me has changed me forever. I can't imagine walking down the streets anymore, as everything looks different from my perspective."

"It does for now, but that will settle down, and it will eventually revert back to normal—whatever that normal will be. In the meantime, we'll do what we can to bring as much normal back to your life as possible."

She smiled at that. "What about your fiancée? Wife?" she asked abruptly. "Is she okay with you being here?"

He stiffened at that, then his shoulders sagged. "Oh, she doesn't give a crap," he admitted, after a moment. "She's already found somebody else, and fortunately she did it just before our wedding day."

She stared at him in horror. "Oh no, I'm so sorry."

He gave her a wry smile. "Yeah, well, it's for the best. So, life has been shitty at my end for a while now."

"Ah, crap." As she thought about what he went through, then she started to get really angry. "Where is that stupid bitch?" she snapped. "I'll have a talk with her." Opal bolted to her feet, staring at him, her hands on her hips. "Where is she? What's her name?"

He stared at her for a moment and then started to chuckle. He snagged her, then tugged her back toward the armchair beside him. "Simmer down. You're not going anywhere and definitely not after her."

"Why not?" she asked. "You're helping me out, and that, at least, is something I can do. You can damn-sure bet I could set that bitch straight. How dare she hurt you like that?"

With the tone of her voice, even Reyes looked over, his lips twitching, almost as if seeing an angry butterfly stand up to a huge killer bee.

Steven shook his head, appreciating the sentiment. "I love you too, sweetheart," he said gently, "but you certainly aren't going after her."

She sat down beside him. "Why not?" She glared at him, and enough belligerence filled her tone that he burst out laughing again.

"Because she's not worth it, and you don't need to get upset about it. I'm obviously much better off without her."

"Oh, you are, indeed. But how could anybody treat you like that?" she repeated in sorrow. "She doesn't understand what she's lost."

"That will be something she finds out later, but not for a while because she's still busily sampling everybody else's wares."

"*Ugh.*" Opal wrinkled up her face. Then she turned on him. "What is your problem that you hooked up with someone like her in the first place?"

At that, Reyes burst out laughing. "I wanted to ask him that same question, but I didn't dare." Reyes was still chuckling. "So I'm really quite delighted that you did."

At that, Steven turned and glared at Reyes. "Really?"

"Oh, absolutely. Those kinds of women, we tend to spot a mile away."

"Apparently I was blind that day. I fell and fell hard," he grumbled, "but I fell for a mirage. So, yeah, I was a fool."

"No, you fell for the whole family dream," Opal corrected him calmly. "I remember you, and I remember all the things you wanted to do and to have. A family with two kids was of prime importance to you, but not until you were ready to settle down. So, she probably lured you in, pretending to believe in your dream, then promptly dropped you when it looked like it might become too real."

He stared at her. "Was I really that set on it?"

"Oh, yes, you were," she murmured. "We talked about it quite a bit."

"Wow, I don't even remember," he murmured, turning his gaze to Reyes and back again.

"I sure do," Opal declared. "At the time I was thinking that it was too damn bad the two of us weren't hooked up"—she smiled—"but we were heading in very different career directions."

"You're right there. I remember having that thought too."

At that, Reyes smiled and shook his head. "Look at you two. Apparently this is old home week. All that is good, but please, can we get on to the business end of things?"

AT THAT, STEVEN and Reyes returned to asking Opal more of the nitty-gritty questions. They continued for a while, until Steven noted Opal was getting tired. Then he got up, walked over, and helped her to stand. "We'll rest on the couch in the living room for a little bit."

She looked up at him. "Why?"

"You'll see." He sat down and then tucked her gently beside him.

She snuggled in close and murmured, "I'm not sure why we're doing this, but it's a really good idea." She was out cold within seconds.

Reyes walked over and sat down on a chair across from him. "She's still incredibly exhausted, isn't she?"

"Yeah, and she won't let herself sleep because of the nightmares," he murmured. All of her ordeal threatened to choke him.

At that, Reyes nodded. "Yet she's completely comfortable with you."

"We were good friends at one time, way back then. And honestly, I'm not her mother, and I'm not a cranky old buzzard that she's known since forever. So, from her perspective, I represent safety, even if only from the current turmoil, because I'm part of her past that was in much happier times."

"Right." Reyes nodded again. "I'll keep working over here on my laptop."

"I'll work here on my phone, so go for it. That she doesn't really know anything is the problem. She can't recognize her tormentors because of the hood. All she can pinpoint, even within the warehouse, was likely Marshal's description, as she never saw it."

"No, and the questions were all about a stash. So where would her father have kept this stash?"

"We're assuming there is one, right?"

"We're assuming that these people had something other than guesswork to go on. So, if they believe there is one, then she's in trouble, whether there is or not."

"Right, and it also depends on who is doing the looking. If drugs are involved, then that stash could be a major deal, and these people won't quit until they find it."

Reyes nodded, a frown forming on his forehead. "And that brings up another set of questions. Just what kind of a bad cop was her father?"

At the same time, Marshal walked in. Hearing the last comment, he replied, "Everything you can think of and all bad. He took bribes, and apparently he arranged for evidence to disappear, even though many safeguards were in place to avoid that happening," he murmured. "I always wondered who was helping him. After Opal was kidnapped, I wondered if her father had a partner, who was looking for the stash they built together."

"Any idea who that could be? How about other friends?"

"That's the thing, as friends go, it's just me," he said bitterly. "I've already been grilled and taken to the cleaners by everybody, and everything has been torn apart. I don't know a damn thing. As far as I can tell, Roscoe was using me as his cover. And the thing is, it worked. As long as I kept protesting his innocence, nobody went any deeper. I was always there for him, all the way. I trusted Roscoe. I was a big, honest, and apparently stupid dupe, who Roscoe used to keep all his other activities protected."

"You have no idea what he might have had as a stash?"

"I didn't even have the slightest clue that he was doing what he was doing, so, no. I don't know where he had a stash or what it would be. I don't even know if there is one. And I don't know who else he could have been working with. You've got to understand that a lot of people could have been, and we interact all the time, so it might have been somebody I know. Yet it might have been somebody from a completely different city. I just don't know."

"That brings up some interesting possibilities too because you're right. Any partner, whether cop or civilian, they don't have to be local, do they?"

"Nope," Marshal confirmed. "And that's something I tried to get the cops to look at, but they were too convinced that I was their guy."

"Which also means that you're being followed by cops and or the guys who kidnapped Opal."

"Every damn day. That's why we rented this house under an assumed name. That's why all the theatrics to get you here today. That's why it's better that you stay here, not at a hotel, to keep down the traveling, so nobody finds our current hidey-hole. I don't even know why the cops still hassle me at this point. And now, with Roscoe dead, you'd think that they would have given up any further investigation. And maybe they have now. My focus is on keeping Opal and Ruby safe. I'm not going out any more than necessary, and I'm not involved in or doing anything in terms of investigating. I'm damn sure not talking to the cops in any way."

"What are you doing for money?" Reyes asked.

"I got to keep my pension. Believe me. They're still trying to strip that from me, but, because they don't have any proof that I was involved in anything, they haven't been able to. And thankfully the union stuck up for me."

"As they should have." Steven stared out the window, keeping still, so Opal slept on. "They can guess all they want, but, without proof, we're still supposed to have due process and a justice system."

"I lost my perspective on the justice system a while ago," Marshal snapped. "Somewhere around the time I found out that my partner and best friend was dirty and had been chumping me for God-only-knows how long."

"And you really don't know who else he might have hung around with?"

"No, I really don't." Marshal shook his head, his glare deepening. "And I get it. I should. I mean, we were friends. We've had plenty of barbecues together and that sort of thing. And I'll admit that one of the draws for being here was Ruby. Maybe Roscoe knew that. I don't know. To be honest, I've always loved her, since forever it seems. Maybe Roscoe knew that too. Maybe he took advantage of that, knowing that it would keep the two of us functioning as partners," Marshal murmured. "I'm so racked with my own guilt over not having seen his crimes that it just pisses me off. I don't know what all he did. I don't know who all he hurt, but I do know he hurt Ruby. And, for me, that's unforgivable."

"And yet, with him gone, at least the field's open for you."

"Honestly, Roscoe going to jail left the field open for me, and she'd already started divorce proceedings but hadn't completed them."

"Right," Steven murmured, "and he wouldn't have contested at that point, I suppose."

"No, he didn't care. He knew the gig was up, and he wasn't getting out anytime soon."

"Do you think he committed suicide?"

"I don't know. I think it's possible. He was definitely an all-in kind of guy. So, if he realized he wasn't getting out on appeals and if this was what his life would be, I can't imagine that life for him. Most of it would have been solitary confinement, what with everyone hating him, guards and prisoners alike. He may very well have decided to cash in his chips, figuring it was a bad deal. He was that kind of a guy."

"Right, so then maybe he wasn't murdered."

"I guess, but, then again, I don't know. I don't know what his life was like in there, but I can imagine it was pretty ugly. Bad cops really have a hard time of it."

"So, where would you suggest we start to look?"

Marshal hesitated, and then he shrugged. "You'll look at it anyway, so, if I were you, and if I didn't know me like I do, I would start with me."

"Which is good," Reyes stated, "because we don't really have much choice. We need to do it regardless."

At that came a cry from the doorway. "He didn't do anything," Ruby snapped. "There's absolutely no reason to investigate his life."

Marshal reached out a hand toward her, and she immediately stepped closer, joining him.

Reyes eyed the two of them. "I get that, but I also know that, from an observer's point of view, it only makes sense to question him first, then rule him out, if we can."

Ruby stared at Reyes, her bottom lip trembling.

Marshal leaned over closer to Ruby and whispered, "It's okay. I would do it if I was them too."

She looked up at him, shook her head, then wordlessly turned and left.

Marshal continued. "You can have access to my phone records, my house, and I'll give you my email log-in." As soon as he walked to the doorway, he added, "I'll send you all the log-ins, and, when you want to go to my place, let me know, and I'll take you there." And, with that, he turned and followed Ruby into the kitchen.

Reyes turned to Steven and raised an eyebrow.

Steven nodded. "That's straightforward enough." He kept his voice low to not wake Opal. "However, I do think we need to rile him up a bit."

"Absolutely," Reyes agreed. "I hate to think of what it would do to the family if he were involved. And yet he is the best suspect. I can't imagine what it's been like for him to find out his partner was a cheat, if Marshal is not involved. It's got to be killing him."

"Exactly. If he is involved, he could be the one looking for the stash." Then, in an even lower voice, he added, "He was also on the spot when they beat her up. And she can't remember or identify either of her kidnappers."

"I'll start digging deeper on him," Reyes stated. "Where do you want to start?"

"Traffic cams," Steven said instantly. "I want to see the feeds from the street cameras from the day she was kidnapped. I want to follow the traffic cams down to the warehouse district in the marina. I don't know if anybody even bothered to look, and I don't want to leave even one stone unturned. All kinds of shit can be found out from that."

"No, I get it," Reyes murmured. "We need to move fast because the days are flying by, and not everybody keeps the videos for long."

Steven nodded, and, when Reyes brought over a second laptop, Steven carefully shifted, so he didn't disturb Opal, yet was able to work on it. He looked down at the sleeping beauty at his side. "I sure hope we can get this solved fast."

"She's healing. Keep that in mind," Reyes suggested. "I get that this is a pretty rough situation, but we are the best hope she's got. Now let's get to work so we can move this forward. Levi will be calling soon to see where we're at."

"*Great.*" Steven gave Reyes an eye roll. "Have fun updating him."

"You mean about the two of you and your relationship? We already knew about it." He grinned.

"Well, hell." He frowned at Reyes. "So that whole matchmaking thing he's got going on is real?" He shook his head, then turned his attention to logging into the networks to get into the traffic cams.

Sometime later Marshal strolled back in again and gave them each a piece of paper with a list of addresses, phone numbers, and log-in information. After seeing what Steven was working on, Marshal asked, "Do you guys have legal access to that stuff?"

"Yeah, sure we do, through Levi."

Marshal hesitated, then nodded. "I guess that's a good thing. It seems odd because that's usually a cop thing."

"It is a cop thing but not only a cop thing." Reyes looked up with a smile. "Besides, somebody needs to be looking into this shit."

"No, I agree," he murmured. "I've lost access to everything. It's not a good feeling when you realize you can no longer access information that once was at your fingertips. Not to mention the part about being considered toxic in the force. All the doors slam shut in my face."

"I get it, but at least you have your pension, and you can leave when you want."

"Yeah, there's that. I'd like to leave. Get a hell of a distance away and not have to deal with any of this anymore," he murmured. "Maybe once we get Roscoe buried, I can, but, at the moment, it's too painful."

"Do you think he would have known anything about what happened to his daughter?"

"If the kidnappers could have told him, I'm sure they would have, just to add to his pain. And maybe he cared. I don't know. I want to think that he did, but … clearly I'm not the best judge." Marshal shrugged.

"How was he?"

"You have to understand. … He wasn't a bad guy. He was just somebody who became singularly focused on what he wanted."

"Even if it hurt other people?" Steven asked.

"I wouldn't have thought so, no, but, from what I've seen now, … the only answer to that is absolutely yes. And that's shitty too because I didn't see that side of him, and it puts everything into question."

"When you say that you were best friends, what did you do on your time off together?"

"Roscoe saw me through a divorce, the loss of a son." Marshal sighed. "I was there for Opal's birth. I was there through a lot of years, when Roscoe got promoted and then demoted," he said, with an eyebrow raised.

"Why was that?" Reyes asked.

"Roscoe was accused of some stuff, but I went to bat for him. After an investigation he was reinstated. He was certainly angry over the whole thing and felt as if nobody had been there for him."

"Except you."

"Except me, and yet, when you're friends, I'm not sure that counts as much, since it was expected."

"Right, and it might have had a part in his motivation to screw over the department that was screwing with his life."

"Maybe, I don't even know anymore," Marshal admitted, his gaze going from one man to the other. "Though I guess that makes a stupid kind of sense. It's not what I would have expected of him. At the same time, Roscoe had changed in the last few years. He was less willing to go out and to do things, more inclined to go home and to spend time with his wife. At least that's what I thought at the time. That racked me over a bit, until I found out, after talking to Ruby, that he had been spending more time away, supposedly with me, and yet neither of us knows to this day where he went." Marshal shook his head.

"You think you know who someone is, after being so close for years, then *boom*. Suddenly you don't know anything, and you can't trust what you thought you knew before." Marshal groaned. "It doesn't matter how many excuses you come up with, you still can't find a way to justify his behavior, and you are left not knowing what to do next."

"Not much you can do," Reyes replied. "His behavior is his behavior. So, is there any chance at all that he was undercover and that he wasn't a bad cop?"

"No, I tried that angle myself. I asked him when I saw him in prison. I kept talking to him about it, trying to get him to tell me what was going on and to give me the truth about who he was working with. Was he undercover? What was his end goal and all that? Because I was certain there had to be one. He flat-out told me that he was done. Done with the department, done with everything. That he wanted to leave his life, and he needed a way to do it. And this was the route he ended up on. I was shocked." Marshal snorted. "Stunned, to put it mildly. It wasn't anything I ever imagined would come out of his mouth."

"Did he ever mention your relationship with his wife?" Steven asked Marshal.

"No, he never did. And let me be clear. Ruby and I didn't have a relationship. That was the thing. As much as I may have wanted her in my life, she was my partner's wife. Therefore, I wouldn't do anything but be a friend to both of them. But I'm pretty sure he knew that I cared about her. I just don't know that he cared enough anymore to give a crap."

"Right," Steven murmured, "so that's another avenue of sorts there."

"I don't know what you can make out of it though," Marshal said. "It's so damn frustrating."

Reyes asked, "What makes you wake up in the morning and decide you're done with your life and want out?"

"Exactly," Marshal replied. "It's quite possibly what happened, but why?"

"Did he see you and his wife together at all?" Steven asked.

"You keep harping on that. Do you really think that had anything to do with it?"

"It makes sense when you think about it because you're there all the time with his wife. And then, if Roscoe was done, didn't want to be married anymore, maybe he figured Ruby would get the house, but Roscoe wanted a nest egg, so he could disappear himself."

Marshal groaned at that. "I don't know. He'd been a straight upstanding guy as far as anybody knew. But, after the prior investigation, he changed."

Steven went silent for a moment. "If you think about it, a deal like that would make anything worse. And, if he thought the department had his back, then found out otherwise, it would be a hard pill to swallow. I'm sure he felt betrayed."

"Which is exactly what I went through," Marshal agreed, "so I know how that feels. It's a betrayal at the deepest levels, and you really don't have any love left in your life for anybody at that point."

"And maybe Roscoe started thinking about taking his wife with him, but then figured she wouldn't go. Maybe he figured she would be happier here, with you. That would cement a decision to leave—knowing you'd be there for her."

Chapter 4

O PAL WOKE UP moaning. A hand gently stroked her face, and she recognized Steven's voice.

"Wake up slowly," he murmured. "You're fine. You're safe. Nobody'll get you."

She shifted so she could look up at him. "I keep sleeping on top of you," she murmured, rubbing her eyes clear of sleep. "I'll need a chiropractor to get my neck back in sync." She sat up slowly and stretched.

He smiled at her. "It's good to see you getting some sleep."

"Little short bouts," she murmured, then yawned. "I'm feeling rather decent. You're good for me."

"In many ways." He chuckled.

"I do remember a lot of good times," she said, shifting to sit beside him. "Remember pizza on the beach?"

"With Madge and Kelly, yeah."

She chuckled. "Whatever happened to those days?"

"We were younger and innocently stupid."

"Hey, you could have left it at young and innocent."

"No, there was definitely some stupid piled in on that," he muttered.

She smiled. "It seems so long ago."

"It *was* a long time ago," he confirmed. "Whether we like it or not, the passage of time has left its stamp on all of us."

"And, for some of us, it's not been very nice," she murmured. "I was doing fine, until this mess happened, and then everything started coming undone."

"You'll be fine again down the road."

"I sure hope so. I want to."

"And you will. Just hold that thought, and don't let anybody sway you from it."

She chuckled. "You sound like a motivational speaker, helping me to get my act together."

"No, not in any way, shape, or form." He stared at her in mock horror. "I understand the struggles and what you've been going through all too well. Unfortunately I've seen cases where people are left with all kinds of trauma to deal with. Eventually you'll be fine. Thankfully you don't have more lasting physical injuries to deal with."

"No, you're right there." She reminded herself how she really should be thankful. She stroked her injured neck gently. "Obviously I wasn't expected to live through this, but to come to terms with the reality that people out there have so little regard for life is scary."

"And again we're back to that loss of innocence," he murmured. "Trust me when I say that you will recover from this. You'll learn some self-defense. You'll learn a few things to make you feel better, to help you sleep at night. And then, at some point in time, you'll realize that things are safer. The realization will likely come as a surprise—but a good one."

"I hope it doesn't take long."

"It seems long but that doesn't mean it's not worth doing."

She smiled at him. "Oh, look. There's that nice man again."

"*Ugh*. Remember? Nobody likes being called nice." He gave her an exaggerated frown. "Next time replace 'nice' with 'sexy.'"

She burst out laughing. "And yet so many men are just nice." She looked over at Reyes. "Look. There's another one."

Reyes lifted his head, his gaze unfocused, then he cleared it, as he stared at her. Suddenly registering her words, Reyes let a huge grin cross his face. "I'm taken. You don't have to worry about me."

She stared at him in confusion, but Steven glared at him. "Ignore him. He's got a twisted sense of humor."

"I like him. He's easy to talk to."

"How would you know?" Steven protested. "You haven't been awake long enough to talk to anybody. Especially not Reyes."

She stared at Steven and then realized the truth of it. "I hadn't really considered that. It just seems like you guys have been here almost forever."

"We haven't. It's only been a few hours."

"No, no, no, I've slept twice, so surely that's two days," she argued, with a mock grin. Slowly she stood, stretched again.

Steven could see the bones starting to show through her wrist. He immediately pulled her wrist gently toward him. "Were you this skinny before?"

She shook her head. "No, but I didn't respond well to the drugs used in the kidnapping or in the hospital either. Plus I was unconscious for quite a while, so I lost a lot of weight. I was quite weak when I got home, but I didn't really think much about it. If you remember, anytime I got sick before, I always dropped a lot of weight. Hopefully I can get past this and heal, then work on regaining some pounds."

"And again it won't be forever," he murmured.

She smiled. "I'd like you to promise me that, but I know you can't do that. It will happen when it happens, and, while I can do the best I can, there's no guarantee."

"Guarantee of what?" Steven asked curiously. "What is it you would like a guarantee of?"

"That it will never happen again." The words flew from her mouth.

"Ah, that makes sense. The chances of it ever happening again are in that *almost impossible* zone. Most people don't survive a true attempted murder, and the chances of it happening twice are pretty slim."

"Pretty slim but not impossible. And it's that *not impossible* that keeps me from sleeping."

"Let us solve this, and then you should be good to go. I don't want you to spend your whole life looking over your shoulder."

She smiled. "In that case, I'll go find some coffee."

He looked at her hopefully. "Times two?"

At that, Reyes lifted his head again, looking over the workstation he'd arranged for himself. "Make that three, please."

She laughed. "Your wish is my command," she replied. Then she headed off in pursuit of coffee. In the kitchen she found her mom and Marshal, holding hands across the table. "Are you two doing okay?"

Her mother hopped to her feet when she saw her, then walked over and gave her the gentlest of hugs. "Hey, you're awake."

"Yeah, I keep sleeping on him. Who knew that, after all this time, I wanted Steven for a pillow?" she joked. Her mom gave her a warm but teary smile. "Mom, I'm getting better, honest."

"I know you are," she whispered. "Honestly, I do. It's all just been so traumatic." It wasn't the same as what her mother had gone through, but it was, in a way. Opal wished she could have saved her mom from this, but then Opal wished she could have saved herself from it as well. "Whoever would have thought that this could happen to us?" Opal asked, not really expecting an answer.

"We've tried hard not to let it affect us and to let go of the baggage and your father's crap," Ruby said, "but I'm not sure we did a good job of it. We did the best we could, but staying out of it all won't be something we're allowed to do now."

"We've tried, but obviously they think we know something."

"Yet you don't, do you?" her mother asked anxiously.

"No, I have no idea what they want." Opal shook her head. "They were talking about a stash, so I presume they think that Dad must have hoarded money, drugs, or something. At this point, I wouldn't be shocked if he had, but I don't know what or where that could be."

Marshal looked over at Opal. "Did he ever give you anything special? Something to hold on to, something that was important to him?"

She shook her head. "No, he sure didn't. He didn't have a whole lot to do with my life in this last little while. He was a good father to me when I was growing up and all, but once he … I don't know. He got …" She stopped, frowned, and finally said, "It's almost as if he got distracted."

"I told the guys that too," Marshal shared, "but I don't know where that's coming from. I don't know in what way it pertains to what's going on."

"If it does at all," Opal added, with a wince. "When we think about it, it's not exactly what we expected from him, but we don't really understand what his more recent behavior was all about. For all we know, he was going through a midlife crisis." She looked over at her mom. "Any chance he knew about you and Marshal?" She hadn't meant to make it sound so bold, but it was well past time for hiding secrets.

Ruby stared at her in shock, then looked at Marshal and back at Opal. "I don't think so. You've got to understand that we weren't *together*, together, not until after he went to prison."

"I get that, but maybe Dad had some indication of where your heart was," she murmured.

"I hope not," Ruby said fervently. "I really do. I wouldn't have done that to him."

"At least not until he did what he did to you," Opal suggested, with half a smile. She didn't mind her mother's relationship with Marshal and hoped her father hadn't known, but, considering the timing, she suspected he had.

Ruby shook her head. "I stuck beside Roscoe until his confession. At that point I realized that I was living a lie with someone who had been lying the whole time. Afterward we never even discussed it. I couldn't. I was too upset."

"Exactly," Opal shared. "And remember. I am an adult, so I do understand a whole lot more than you might realize. Don't try protecting me from anything."

"There wasn't anything," her mother protested. "That's the problem. If I could have said, 'Hey, we had a big fight, and I told Roscoe to leave and that I wanted to spend the rest of my life with Marshal,' then at least there would have been an incident to point to. There would be a reason for what Roscoe did. But he started all this so much earlier, and, as to what or why honestly, I have no clue."

"Good enough." Opal nodded. "I didn't hear any mention of you or Marshal during the beating, but then I wasn't cognizant of everything. For all I know, I was just next on some list, and I couldn't have told them anything anyway. I think they loved their job a little too much."

"And they won't get you again," Marshal said instantly, his tone harsh.

She gave him a sad smile. "If we don't solve this, there's absolutely no way to know that for sure. You can't protect us twenty-four hours a day forever, and we can't live that way either."

"No, but we must stay safe." Marshal's tone was harsh. "We can't all look over our shoulders every day for the rest of our lives."

"Maybe not," Ruby agreed, "but I'm not sure what else we're supposed to do. I just want to go away, where we can't be found—somewhere safe."

"You brought in Levi's men," Marshal noted, "and, if there's one thing I know for sure, it's that Steven will make sure that Opal is safe. He won't let anything else happen to her."

"But can he stop it?" Opal murmured. "I get this is what he does, and honestly, it blows me away and yet tickles me at the same time, but there is also no guarantee that I'll be safe just because he's here."

"No, that's true, but, at least as far the kidnappers know, you're dead. A new ID, a new apartment in a new city, all that takes you away, keeps you safe."

Opal groaned. "A new life doing what? I lose my schooling and have to start over." She sighed. "And yet that's a good thing," she murmured, "for now. How sad to think that I had to die to be safe."

"And yet it's the best possible outcome. And, if we need to"—Marshal stared from one woman to another—"we can get a whole new life for you somewhere else."

She stared at him. "You mean, like stay dead?"

He nodded slowly. "Believe me. I've thought of it," Marshal admitted. "I do know people who can set up new identities. Obviously there's no witness protection for you because your dad was who he was." Marshal's tone turned bitter. "However, we could move to Mexico, and you could start all over again. We all could."

She stared at him, her heart pounding, as she thought about all that would mean. "I'm not sure that they wouldn't follow us there," she responded slowly. "And that's a disconcerting thought as well."

"Maybe, but we'd have an easier chance of disappearing down there than up here."

Opal nodded reluctantly. "Let's see what these guys can come up with, before we take such drastic action."

"I hear you. I just don't know how long they'll need, and I want you to be safe."

She smiled at Marshal. "Thank you for that, and did I ever thank you properly for rescuing me?"

He laughed. "I don't know whether you did or not, but believe me. I don't need to hear it. When the doc saw them throw you overboard and told me that you were unconscious and more or less drowning as you sank, I didn't even have the words." Even now, he was choked up at the thought.

She smiled. "You're the one who kept me alive and got me to the surface. I also owe that doctor a debt I can never repay."

"That's the last thing he wants," Marshal murmured. "He really doesn't want anybody to know that he had anything to do with it. Just like me, he's perfectly aware that whatever was going on was bad news, and, if he gets involved, he could end up deep-sixed, as you were."

"I always thought that was some bad joke from the movies. Who knew people actually do that shit."

"They shouldn't obviously. That's a shitty way to live or die. And hopefully that's not something we'll ever see again, but, yeah, it happens."

She nodded. "It's pretty stupid. Of all the things that people could do with their life, these guys are busy tossing people overboard."

He chuckled. "Now you have a whole new opportunity to see what you want to do with your life because now you get a second chance. You're alive, and nobody knows it, so what do you want to do?"

She studied him thoughtfully for a long moment. "I have no clue, but I can tell you one thing right now. I want coffee."

"You're such a baby," Ruby teased, then burst out laughing.

With her mother and Marshal chuckling behind her, Opal put on the coffee, her mind wandering at the ideas that had been brought up. As Marshal suggested, running might be her only chance, but did she want to be on the run forever? Did she want to take off and have to recreate her life into something new and different?

She was almost done with her job anyway. Now, if only her degree was complete, it would be a whole different story. She wasn't sure of the next course of action, but she made a mental note to talk to the school very quickly. Everything was hanging on what Steven could find out regarding her dad and her recent kidnapping. Yet, at the same time, it was hard to care about continuing her education. It was hard to think of anything but what had gone wrong in her world.

That was slowing down her own mental processes too. She understood that, to Marshal, this was a case of *let's up and disappear*, but she didn't want to run. Opal didn't want to go through such an upheaval. She wanted this solved, and she wanted people to know that she had nothing to do with her father's issues and that they should leave her alone. She didn't know what that would take though. The last thing she wanted was to have her mother targeted next.

So much shit was going on, so much craziness. Opal didn't understand how these guys were getting away with what they did. However, at the same time, was anybody still even looking for her? Or, as with her father's death, was everybody happy that she was gone, so they could move forward in life and not worry about it?

And who would look? Her friends were told she'd been in an accident, her school that she was sick. Her apartment lease canceled, … as if she'd already died.

That also brought up Opal's feelings of guilt. After all the shit her dad pulled, he was still her father, and, in some ways, knowing he was dead was a relief. However, at the same time, it made her feel horribly guilty. Neither had she taken time to grieve. Her healing was taking a lot out of her. Her sleep issues made it hard to function sometimes. Talk about being a mess. But since her father was essentially responsible for what happened to Opal, it was hard to find any forgiveness in her heart and soul for him.

She knew that fact alone would keep her in trouble, and

it would be something that crippled her, if she couldn't find a way to get past it. Was it really a case of just the eventual passage of time? Was it possible that Steven was correct? In that case, she was already working on it.

She wanted to live her life, her old peaceful life. What would it take to get that back? Everything now was still so screwed up. She was a prisoner in her own house. A ghost to the outside world.

"How fair was that?" she murmured to herself. Of course it wasn't fair at all, and nobody gave a crap. Well, other than the four people here with her and some related people she only knew by name: Levi, Ice, Ice's doctor dad. It was what it was, and Opal would deal with the aftermath.

When the coffee was ready, she poured three cups, as requested, then looked over at her mother and Marshal. "There's fresh coffee, if you want some," she murmured. Then, leaving the two of them alone, she headed back to the living room.

Even though her mom's relationship with Marshal was out in the open, it confused her. She'd seen it before they admitted to seeing each other and hadn't had a problem with it. She knew her mother had desperately needed somebody to get through this nightmare, but it was one more thing that was out of kilter in Opal's world, which made her feel worse.

That made no sense, and she knew it. She didn't know what she could do about any of it. Maybe there was absolutely nothing to be done; maybe this is what her world was now. That brought tears to her eyes, as she thought about it, because she'd never imagined her life going in this direction. And feeling sorry for herself would not get her any awards.

Not only would it not get her any awards, it also wouldn't do her any good. That horse had left the barn, and she was stuck with the reality of whatever it was that she could deal with now. When she delivered the coffee, she was very aware of two intense gazes staring at her. She attempted a smile. "Hey, any progress?"

"We're getting there. How are you holding up?" Steven got up and retrieved a mug of coffee from the tray she'd brought.

"Not very well," she murmured, "but that's probably not unexpected." Steven nodded and didn't say anything. She liked that about him. He was really easy to talk to and had always been there for her—if he knew that she needed somebody, that is, but she hadn't even known that she did. It made her feel odd to think that he'd come at a time when she had needed him so desperately.

She didn't know whether that was fate or if there was a power above, but she was damn grateful for it. She would have to send Levi a personal email, thanking him for sending Steven. And she couldn't imagine what her life would be like right now without them. She sat down on the couch beside Steven, just as she had before.

He looked at her with a wry smile. "Ready for another nap?"

She chuckled. "I should be, but I think I'll be good for a little bit."

"As soon as you need to." And he patted his shoulder.

"I shouldn't be depending on you so much. I should be capable of handling it myself."

He immediately stopped her with his finger against her lips. "There's a time for that. You can worry about progress later, but right now you must get your strength back, and you have to heal. In order to heal, you must sleep."

She smiled. "Thank you, *Doctor*. I was feeling guilty for

taking advantage."

He burst out laughing. "You can take advantage of me anytime," he said, flashing her a wicked grin.

She loved that they had fallen back to the same old easy camaraderie they had had before. "I'm really sorry we lost touch. I probably could have told you that woman was totally wrong for you."

"You probably could have," he agreed calmly, "but I might not have listened."

"No, you never were very smart. Headstrong, stupid, and bullish, but smart? No."

"Hey," he protested. "Be nice."

She looked at him but felt a lightness in her heart. "Yeah, not happening now."

And he burst out laughing, leaned over, and gave her a gentle kiss on the lips.

She smiled. "It's really good to have you back here."

"It is. I'm sorry that it took this to bring me back into your world."

"Me too. So let's make sure that, when this is over, we're not such strangers anymore."

"I'd love that. I'd forgotten how good it is to have you around."

"Me too," she murmured. "It seems life sends you down that busy pathway, and you get so involved with things that constantly distract you, and, before you know it, years have gone by, and you've lost touch with everybody who was important at one time."

"How is that even possible? I did it too," Steven admitted. "We were close. We were really close."

"We were, and we still are."

"That is something that blows me away now too. We

still are close, and yet we aren't. All that time went by, when we could have been texting or emailing or something. And yet we didn't. Why is that?"

"Everybody gets busy. Everybody gets distracted and involved. Before you know it, months have gone by."

"Sure, months at first, and those months became nine years or so for us."

She stared at him. "I'd like those years back. I want a do-over."

At that, Reyes burst out laughing. "When you two have figured out how to make that happen, let me know because plenty of other people want a do-over too."

She faced him and nodded. "Right, there should be a point in time where we get to punch a button and stop for a moment, saying, 'I want to sit here and reanalyze how far I've come and where I'm going and whether I'm happy with this path,' in case you might want to change it," she murmured. "With my do-over, I never would have walked home from work that day."

"Honestly, that wouldn't have made any difference," Steven noted, bumping her gently on the nose. "Because they would find you at home, on the way home, at work, whatever. This way, at least nobody else was hurt."

She stared at him, and then her face twisted into a wry frown. "Why hadn't I considered that?"

He slipped an arm around her shoulders and hugged her gently. "Hey, go easy on yourself. You've been to hell and back," he murmured. "There's no one way to get all these answers ahead of time. What happens, happens, and we deal with it the best we can."

"Yeah, but it didn't happen to you," she cried out painfully.

He cupped her cheeks with his hands. "No, it didn't. It happened to you. And that's why we're all working so hard to make sure it doesn't happen again."

She sank back into the couch, staring at her own mug on the coffee table in front of them. "I feel as if I could have done something."

"And what could you have done?" Steven asked curiously.

"I don't know. Yet I feel as if an answer is there. Maybe I should have given them something that would have stopped them from taking that final terrible path."

"I don't think it would have made a damn bit of difference," Steven argued, his tone harsh. "You knew too much at that point. Once they snagged you, you were already a goner. However, the good news is, you survived." And he gently ran a finger down her throat. "And that is worth everything."

She winced, and he immediately withdrew his fingers.

She shook her head. "You didn't hurt me. It's just that reminder."

"A reminder that never goes away."

She nodded. "How fair is that?"

"Love and life are not fair," he reminded her.

"You used to say shit like that all the time. It was just as irritating back then too." He burst out laughing, and she grinned at him. She turned to Reyes. "Sorry, are we bugging you?"

"No, I'm working away."

At that, she frowned at him. "Right, and I'm taking you both away from work, so go on, get back to work." She waved her hand at the two of them. "I'll sit here and recuperate."

"You do that. No more distractions." Steven tossed her a

71

big grin.

"I couldn't distract you if I tried," she scoffed. "You were always like that. Once you got into something, you were a terrier and wouldn't stop until you solved it."

He glanced over at her. "Every time you open your mouth, I stop and listen."

She immediately pinched her lips together, then said, "Fine." Yet she glared at him, then chuckled, realizing how much time the two of them had missed together. Something she didn't want to have happen again.

He went back to his laptop. Out of the corner of her eye, she caught sight of his screen. When she saw what happened, she gasped. He looked over at her. "Yes, I'm checking the traffic camera systems," he noted.

Her breath let out in a *woosh*. "I didn't even think that was something you could check."

"I can. I want to know what they did, what vehicle they took you in, and whether I can track it."

She watched in amazement as he fiddled with the video in another program. And then he latched onto the still photo of the dark van that she had been immediately pulled into. She knew what was going on inside that van, and it caused her pain. "Damn, it hurts to see it happen."

But, at the same time, she also knew it was a good thing that he was looking at it. She didn't want to, but then he brought up something different on the screen, and she heard his soft and deadly voice.

"Aha."

She looked over at him and then leaned closer, so she could see what it was he was excited about. And there, from a completely different video, he was looking at the same van. "I don't know what that was all about," she said crossly. "I thought maybe you'd magically found something."

"I did," he murmured.

She looked at him and back at the screen. "It's still the same van."

Then he tapped the screen and the license plate.

She stared at it and finally got what that meant. "Oh my God." She bolted upright, standing on her feet. "Can you find them now?"

"Let's just say, we are a whole lot closer," he murmured. He pulled off a screenshot of that license plate and sent it to Levi. "Now we'll keep following them via this video feed and see if I can figure out where they go."

As she watched, completely fascinated, he kept following video after video, losing the vehicle, then finding it again. "I don't understand. Why didn't the cops do this?"

"Maybe they would have, if you had been reported as missing. Or maybe they wouldn't, if it were another bad cop involved," he stated, his gaze intent on the moving screens. "What I don't know is how many people were aware of what happened to you."

"Seriously I don't know either. Marshal didn't seem to think anybody would listen. And maybe he's right. Maybe they wouldn't."

Steven nodded, as he watched the screen, as vehicle after vehicle moved on by.

Then suddenly she stabbed at the laptop. "There it is again."

"Yeah, I see it." Then Steven switched to a whole different view.

"Are you following all the street cameras?"

"Until I can track where he goes, yes."

Such a sense of determination filled his voice that she

realized how important this was to him. And how lucky she was to have him on her case. She sagged against him and whispered, "Thank you for coming."

He leaned over, kissed her gently on her temple. "I would have been here sooner, if I'd known."

"I realize that now. It never even occurred to me to contact you. I was in so deep that I knew I wouldn't survive. Mom made the call."

"For that," Steven whispered, "we'll always be grateful because now I'm here. And don't worry. We'll get to the bottom of this." For the first time she realized he was absolutely serious. He was determined to get to the bottom of it.

NOW THAT STEVEN had something tangible to track, he wouldn't lose it. He had to backtrack several times, and, somewhere in his distant peripheral vision, he realized that she was watching his every move. She was just as fascinated with the process as he was. Also it was the first time she was really seeing what had happened to her. He had found that, because the victims experienced the event from a completely different perspective, in some cases they never got to see how shocking the event was.

He didn't want Opal to have more nightmares. It was bad enough for him to know what she had gone through, in theory. His mind could conjure up all the details just fine. Seeing her terror at the initial kidnapping event had been bad enough, but she'd survived so much worse after being snatched. These assholes hadn't given her any chance. Not only that, they had deep-sixed her as soon as they could, even though she'd never been without a hood and could in no way have ID'd them.

For that, they would pay.

Steven didn't know what way or shape or manner that would take. He would ensure that whatever happened, happened for the right reasons. He wasn't about to throw away his whole life, not now that he had her back in it.

Who knew that Steven had a gaping hole being filled right now with her, as if she belonged? Had always belonged? He didn't quite understand this need to be with her right now, except that he was a compassionate person who cared very much about her.

Yet, at the same time, he knew that there was more to it than that, but Steven had no time to process this new revelation, had no time to do anything but hunt her kidnappers and would-be killers. And this is what he loved to do best.

When his phone rang, he snatched it up. "Hello."

"That vehicle was stolen two nights before her kidnapping."

"Of course it was," Steven said in disgust, hearing the same tone in Levi's voice. "And I suppose there's no video camera footage or anything regarding the theft, is there?"

"No, there isn't," Levi confirmed. "However, the same vehicle is also suspected to have been used in a bank robbery ten years ago."

"What? And yet it was stolen?"

"Supposedly stolen a couple years ago too."

"That makes no sense."

"Right. After being used in a robbery a decade earlier, it was sold off in a police auction. And it was stolen twice since then."

"Or somebody from ten years ago decided they wanted

their van back because it was good luck?"

Levi chuckled. "We've seen all kinds of shit, so that's not outside the realm of possibilities."

Steven added, "Well, I also have the traffic cameras footage up, and I'm following that vehicle through the streets, and we're definitely heading toward the marina. We have the address of the warehouse from Marshal himself. I'm checking to see whether the van is going straight there or if it's heading somewhere else. No, it's veering off." He swore. "Jesus, they went to a fast-food joint."

"Really?"

"Yeah, I guess even assholes need to eat." Beside him, Steven sensed Opal being strangely quiet. He reached over a hand. "So far, we're getting a lot of details, but we haven't gotten anything concrete for motive. It is possible they were looking for a stash of some kind. Either drugs or money. And I'm wondering if we are looking at a partner in crime here, who had insider knowledge of the stash in the first place."

"Interesting," Levi said. "And yet you're not thinking it was his police partner?"

"Reyes is hunting through all that. Marshal's been pretty forthcoming with a ton of information, so suspicion is there, of course, but nothing points in that direction as of yet."

"Which is also a good way to clear himself."

"I know." Steven kept his voice calm and low, so as not to get anybody too interested in what was going on. Still, Opal stared at him in surprise, but he didn't say anything.

"Let me know if you come up with anything else," Levi said, before ending the call.

Steven looked over at Reyes. "Reyes, get this. The kidnap vehicle was stolen ten years ago, before being used in an unsolved armed robbery. Thereafter it was sold during the police auction some five years ago and then stolen two more times, once two years ago and then the second time just two days before kidnapping Opal."

Reyes looked at him. "Seriously?"

"Yeah, seriously."

"What do you want to bet that the armed robbery is connected."

"It makes sense."

"How does that make sense?" she asked in confusion.

"Maybe it's a bad luck vehicle. Or maybe somebody used it because it was a good luck vehicle."

She stared at him and then got it. "Meaning that because they got away with the bank robbery in that set of wheels, they wanted it back again?"

"Or they knew where it ended up. Or maybe they bought it themselves, so they would have it available."

"But it was stolen."

"It's pretty easy to make it seem to be stolen because all you have to do is report it missing. The cops don't have any other way of knowing, and then you use it yourself."

"Oh, wow, that's stupidly ingenious."

The two men looked at her. Reyes spoke up. "The thing about crime is, you try to make it as simple as possible. The minute you start making it complicated, … something gets screwed up, and you can't get anywhere near a clean getaway. Then, when you have to start lying, everything you lie about ends up coming back to haunt you."

She nodded slowly. "I can see that. Even trying to get away with shit growing up, the minute you lie, you have to remember your lies."

"In which case," Reyes explained, "most of the lies get

caught, and, once you're caught in one lie, nobody'll believe anything else you say."

Steven agreed. "Which is why detectives work so hard to break down all the information that they're told, when they get it in an interview."

In a low voice she asked, "Are you seriously looking into Marshal?"

"Yes, we're seriously looking into Marshal," he declared calmly. "And Marshal willingly handed over all his information for that reason."

She didn't know what to think of that, and Steven could tell from her facial expression.

He smiled. "We have to. We aren't doing a good job and covering all our bases if we don't look into your father's partner."

"And that's why the department did it too, isn't it?"

"Absolutely," he murmured. "You weren't the only victim. Marshal was too."

"Right. I can't even imagine what that must have felt like for him."

"I can't imagine it either," Steven said, "but you know more than anyone because that's also what happened to you."

"Everything is such a shit show."

He chuckled. "It is, but we're on top of this, and we're making some progress now."

She smiled. "I'm really glad to hear that. I don't even know what to think about any of this anymore."

"And it's not for you to worry about. You focus on healing."

She nodded. "But it's pretty hard to have an empty mind. Every time I close my eyes, I see the same damn thing."

"Of course you do, and, if you remember anything else, be sure and tell me. Other than that, relax, watch some TV, do anything that you want to do. But don't contact anyone, okay?"

"Right," she winced. "Hard to explain any of this to people I know."

"Maybe they aren't involved or suspicious, but what we don't want is for the media to find out that you're alive and or, even worse, for the media to find out what happened to you."

"I guess that would be the worst-case scenario, wouldn't it?"

"Yes, absolutely," he murmured. "They will take the news global. Letting everyone see you're alive and survived the attack would just let know the kidnappers know that they failed, making them even more dangerous."

"Right. Not exactly what we want right now."

"No, absolutely not," he murmured.

She sat here, sipping her coffee, watching as he worked. He was aware of her but kept that knowledge out of the way, so as to not be so disturbing.

He followed the truck on the videos back to the warehouse. He checked the time stamps, then waited for the vehicle to move again, trying hard to ignore what was going on inside that warehouse, where she had been held captive. As soon as she was led out to the vehicle, he checked the time stamp again.

"They had you for four hours, so it was a relatively fast scenario."

She stared at him. "If that is supposed to make me feel better, it's not working."

"It's not meant to make you feel better at all. It means that they were also very aware of the time element."

She thought about that and shrugged. "It's not as if anybody would have reported me missing."

"No, and maybe they knew that. Maybe they knew that you were going out with a girlfriend that night."

"But, even if I hadn't canceled, it's not as if my friends would have been too bothered. They would have texted me a few times, then given up, expecting to talk to me the next day."

"Who were you going out with?"

"One of the other techs that I went to school with. And I doubt she was involved in any way."

"That doesn't mean she doesn't know somebody who knows somebody though. Has she phoned or tried to contact you?"

"I don't think so, but someone did text her, and I think it was from Mom, saying that I canceled because I wasn't feeling well. And then, when I didn't show up for work the next day, Mom told her that I was in a car accident."

"For the moment, we'll keep her out of it but might need to contact her later."

"I'd appreciate that."

"Did she work at the same office? In the same position?"

She nodded. "Yes. We were both hired at the same time. We were also classmates."

"So, she's handling your job right now."

"Yes, that would make sense. We weren't terribly busy, so the fact that I'm not there is something that unfortunately they might be totally okay with." Her voice faded, as she seemed to realize, once again, that her future, her plans, her *everything* had been affected by this.

"We'll sort it out when we get there," Steven told her. "It's not time to worry about that."

She looked over at him and smiled. "Right, so *don't get ahead of myself* is what you're saying."

"Absolutely. That's exactly what I'm saying. You need to look after yourself first. Your future second."

Chapter 5

W HILE THE MEN worked, Opal napped several more
times. By the time evening rolled around, she still felt
as if they were no further ahead—except her frame of mind,
now rested and reassured at Steven's presence, felt calmer, for
the first time since the incident. It was dark outside, and she
knew she had to go to bed soon. And felt her hard-won sense
of peace disintegrating. She hadn't been stolen from her bed,
yet, at the same time, she also knew that she would be
separated from Steven—her security blanket.

When it looked impossible to avoid, she said *Good night*
to everybody, slowly dragging her feet upstairs, hating every
step. Since she'd regained consciousness, her nights were one
long terrifying ordeal. When she heard Steven call out
behind her, she turned to see him striding up the stairs.
"What's the matter?" she asked.

"You. Come on. Let's go." And he took the stairs two at
a time. She raced up ahead of him. "You're still petrified.
Have you even slept in here yet?"

She shook her head. "I've come up every night but haven't managed an hour's sleep here yet. Not only is it *not* my
room," she added, in a wry smile, "but the nightmares start
as soon as I'm alone in the dark."

"I know," Steven whispered, "so I'll stay in here until
you fall asleep."

She stared at him, feeling relief wash over her. "Really?"

"Yes. Remember what I said? There's a time and a place to be strong, and this isn't it. You need to heal. You need to get yourself back in control and back on track. So go get ready for bed."

As she headed to the bathroom, she was smiling, realizing that he was serious. That warmed her heart all over again. It felt dangerous to rely on him, but the fact that he understood was pretty amazing. When she came back out, dressed in old-fashioned pajamas, both the top and the bottoms, he looked up and chuckled.

"You look like a three-year-old."

"I almost feel that way," she muttered. "Especially right now."

"Whatever makes you feel better," he said firmly. "Hold off on the judgment."

She nodded. "That's such an odd thing though," she murmured. "But having you around, I feel a hell of a lot safer."

"Good, wow. Just don't start thinking about the *what ifs* when I'm gone. Because I promise, I'll come back. I'm here until this is solved."

"Good. Otherwise I might just kidnap you myself and keep you here."

He burst out laughing. "Come on. Get into bed."

"What will you do? Read me a bedtime story?"

"Nope, that's not happening. However, I will sit here and work on my laptop, while you sleep."

"Is that a good idea?" she murmured, as she burrowed under the covers, while he hopped in atop the covers and leaned against the headboard and settled the laptop on his lap.

"It's a great idea." He smiled at her reassuringly. "Now get to sleep."

So, she rolled over, certain that, even with his presence, she wouldn't fall asleep. And yet, to her surprise, she found herself sleeping solidly, until she woke up in the middle of the night, wide awake, her heart slamming against her chest, fighting the bedding in terror. She gasped several times, as she recognized her room, now sagging back down onto the bed. Checking the clock, she noted it was three in the morning.

She got up and went to the bathroom. She knew a night of tossing and turning was ahead of her. Hearing an odd sound in the house below, she froze and tiptoed to the door, until she heard Steven's voice.

"Yeah, I'll go up and check on her."

She immediately raced back into bed, not sure whether she should be delighted or worried. And what was that inner instinct that he had, which told him that she was awake? Just like a parent. She didn't know whether she should try to fake it or not, but, when he popped open the door and stuck his head around, she called out to him softly, "I'm awake."

"For how long?" he asked, coming in.

She yawned. "Only a few minutes. A nightmare woke me up. Then I went to the bathroom and came back to bed. I was about to come down, when I heard voices downstairs."

He nodded. "That was me. I was changing shifts."

She frowned. "What do you mean, *you're changing shifts?*"

"We're running shifts, security shifts, to make sure somebody's always awake and alert."

"Really?" She hadn't even been aware of that. "I might have been able to sleep on my own, if you had told me that."

"Not likely," he disagreed cheerfully. "Besides, it's what we nearly always do."

She chuckled. "You've hardly even worked for Levi long enough to know what you *always* do."

His teeth flashed white in the darkness, as he smiled at her words. "The particular boss doesn't matter. Some things are universal in my line of work. That is definitely universal."

"Wow," she murmured, "so it's your watch right now then?"

"It is, so get back to sleep again."

She didn't even know what to say, but she already felt her eyelids sinking heavily against her cheeks. "I don't want to sleep late," she murmured.

"Sleep is what you need," he protested.

"But I don't want the days to disappear on me so fast that I lose track."

"I don't think that will happen," he said simply. "Close your eyes and rest."

And, with that, knowing he was here, she drifted off again.

STEVEN STAYED IN her room, working at her side for a few hours, then tiptoed out, making sure that she didn't wake up from his movements. With her sound asleep, he headed back down, checking through the kitchen and the living room to make sure all was silent.

Marshal had left earlier, but still quite late, as Ruby had been hard-pressed to relax. So far, Reyes hadn't found anything of concern in Marshal's background. However, because of Marshal's position as Roscoe's partner, it would be hard to discount him, without a proper investigation.

Marshal had too much access to Roscoe's family and previous life. And the fact that Marshal was trying to talk Ruby and Opal into leaving the country added to it. Steven and Reyes didn't want Marshal to be the bad guy, didn't want him to be involved in any way at all, but what if Marshal had found the stash? What if he knew his partner well enough to pinpoint where or what that stash was? It wouldn't be shocking if he didn't want to share it because he had taken a terrible hit from all of this too.

Once Marshal had left, Steven had voiced his suspicions to Reyes, who nodded in agreement. "I was thinking that too. I don't want him to be that guy, but it's hard to not think along those lines."

"Exactly, and what do we think about the rescue?"

"I think it's too damn convenient," Reyes said bluntly. "At the same time, if he hadn't been there, we know she'd be dead."

"If she was *that* close," Steven stated, "we need to talk to the doctor. His name is here, but I suggest we don't call him now, as he's working a night shift," Steven said, looking at the sheet before him. "Maybe I should call him during his shift." Later on, he did and left a message, when there was no immediate answer. Later, when Steven wandered through the house, his phone rang, and he realized it was the doctor. He hurried into the kitchen, where nobody could hear him, then answered it. When he identified himself, the doctor sighed.

"I really didn't want to get involved."

"I understand that. Believe me. We'll try to keep you out of this as much as possible. However, I need you to corroborate what we've been told."

"Is Marshal a suspect?"

"No, not necessarily, but, if we can rule him out, that

allows us to focus on what really happened."

"That always pisses me off," the doctor grumbled. "The good guys are the ones who get the shit. And I'm pretty sure he's taken enough shit over this whole deal to want to give up and to walk away from it all."

"I imagine he does."

"He's a good guy though. I've known him for a long time."

"So, can you tell me the events of that evening, please?" With a heavy sigh, the doctor repeated what had happened from his perspective, and it did line up exactly with Marshal's account of the narration. "Did Marshal give you any explanation of what was going on, prior to seeing Opal dumped overboard?" Steven asked the doc.

"He was frantic, saying they were trying to kill somebody. My boat was already in the water. I'd had it out, and I knew the area well. I was on my fishing day, and his request didn't go over so well, but whatever," he murmured. "Sometimes you have to do what you have to do."

"You're in the business of saving lives." Steven smiled. "I don't imagine you expected to save one this way."

"Honestly, I didn't think she'd make it. She was in really rough shape. But resilience is an incredible thing, and the human body has an unbelievable compulsion for survival." The doctor paused. "How is she doing?"

"Nightmares are a problem, and her throat's still very sore, but she's able to talk a little bit and is able to remember bits and pieces."

"That's too bad." The doc sighed. "For her sake, I was hoping she wouldn't remember anything."

"She doesn't remember or have any cognitive awareness of being thrown overboard," he murmured.

"That's a blessing. That was an incredible thing for them to do to her. I couldn't believe it myself, and I've seen too much of what humans do to each other, but that? Jesus."

Steven heard the horror still filling the doctor's tone. "Oh, I agree. I agree entirely."

"Anything else?" the doctor asked distractedly. "I've got to get back to work."

"No, that lines up with Marshal's story."

"Of course it does. I told you. He's a good man." And, with that, the doctor rang off.

Feeling better about that, Steven made notes of the conversation, sent them off to Levi as an email, with a copy to himself and to Reyes. They needed to keep track of everything they possibly could. Steven still wanted to go to Marshal's house, and he would do that regardless of how the women felt about it, so Steven could clear Marshal.

The trouble was, Steven also knew that Marshal had already had plenty of time to clear out his house too. But still, due diligence required that they at least check it out.

Marshal knew that as well, which also made for a strange situation, when your suspect was fully aware of what you were doing. Yet, when Steven thought about what it would have been for Marshal to find out what his partner had done, and to know that everybody in the cop shop would treat Marshal differently forever—and judge him for it as well—it must have been hard to endure, if not impossible.

Even when Steven found that his own fiancée was cheating on him, and he promptly broke off the engagement, a lot of people didn't believe him. A lot of people felt as if he'd done wrong to force her to go in that direction. Maybe he did; he didn't know. All he'd tried to do was be a good person and to be there for her. But, whatever he'd done, it hadn't been enough.

Even now, as he sat here wondering, all he could think about was how ending his engagement had been a complete reprieve because he wouldn't have been happy in that relationship for long. He didn't think that she was capable of fidelity. If she'd already been out playing games, as they got closer to the wedding date, no way she would have been honest and true during the marriage.

And it occurred to him that maybe she couldn't tell him that she was unhappy and how she wanted to break it off, and so cheating had been her way. He'd heard of things like that happening. He didn't see how or why somebody would pull a stunt like that. It would be so much easier to just be honest and upfront, but maybe he was scarier than he thought. Maybe talking to him was something she wasn't capable of doing. He frowned at that because it didn't make him feel very good, but what did he know?

Obviously he didn't have any problems with Opal, but then they knew each other from a long time ago. And yet still, it was as if the years had disappeared instantly. He really loved that about her. The fact that he'd always been able to talk to her was a help, but even now, after so much time apart, it seemed to be a gift that he hadn't even recognized back then. A gift he hadn't realized he'd needed, not until she was stolen off the street, beaten up, and tossed over-board—now completely traumatized by what these assholes had done to her. So much so that he didn't know what she'd even be like down the road. He could only hope that she'd make a full recovery. If somebody like him were around in her life, then maybe she could find her way back again.

He wasn't by any means egotistical, but he also knew that his attitude would not let her get away with hiding. She had so much to offer the world. He would want her to reclaim her full potential. But that recovery would take time, would exact a cost, and would require something she had in spades. *Resilience.*

It was too easy to hide in this life. Too easy to distance yourself from the pain and then distance yourself right out of life in a way. That wouldn't help her; it wouldn't make her happy or fulfilled in any way. To have her feeling as if life was something she wanted to live, yet couldn't, was the worst. Or even worse would be to find out she had committed suicide because she couldn't live with all the memories that were crowding in her head.

That was not something he wanted to hear down the road. In that moment, he realized that no way would that happen because he wouldn't let it. He wouldn't let her out of his sight for a moment. He knew Reyes saw something more there that Steven hadn't really been looking at either.

When he heard a cry from upstairs, he knew that she was awake again. He bolted up the steps, only to find her tossing and turning on the bedding, caught up in a nightmare.

"No, no," she cried out. "I didn't do anything. I didn't."

It seemed that whatever was going on was so traumatizing that she couldn't seem to shake it, even in the nightmare. He pulled back the covers and woke her.

Still, she cried out, "No, no, leave me alone, leave me alone."

He felt the pain in his own heart as he realized she thought Steven was an attacker, but of course she did. The fact that he was only here to help wouldn't matter to her subconscious. As he softly took her shoulders in his hands, she cried out, "I don't know who you are. I don't know what you want."

"Opal."

"I don't know anything." Then her head snapped to the side, as if she were being beaten.

He immediately shook her awake, his heart breaking. "It's okay," he murmured. "It's okay."

She took one look at him and then burst into tears. "Oh my God," she cried out. "Make it stop."

But he knew there was no way that he could. Some of these things had to work their way through her psyche in their own time. And maybe her mind was trying to tell her something, or maybe it was just a warning that everything out there was dangerous. He held her close, and she curled into his body, sobbing giant sobs that tore at his heart.

"One of them is called John," she whispered suddenly. "I heard the other guy say something like, 'John, she doesn't know anything.'"

"That's good. Anything else?" Steven couldn't see her features in the dark. The curtains were closed, so not even moonlight filtered in.

She shook her head. "It doesn't really help though, does it?" she asked bitterly. "What difference does it make if it's John or not?"

"Every name helps. Every name is a nail in their coffin."

"And yet it's my coffin they were trying to fill." She started to bawl.

And there wasn't a whole lot Steven could do but hold her close.

Chapter 6

OPAL WOKE THE next morning alone, yet feeling surprisingly rested. And, for that, she knew she had Steven to thank. He'd stayed with her after she woke up with that most recent nightmare. But she also had that weird sense of having brought a name out of her subconscious. And while that did feel funny, it also felt good, as if she were doing something to help herself.

"Hey, if this helps them find whoever did this, then perfect," she murmured. And here she was, still caught up in it all, still fighting for answers. She got up, had a shower, and slowly made her way downstairs. Marshal wasn't there, and neither was Reyes.

She looked over at Steven. "Where did Reyes go?"

"He went with Marshal to his house."

She winced at that. "Gosh, I wish you guys would leave that man alone."

"We will when our investigation into Marshal is done." Steven smiled, not giving an inch. She glared at him. His grin widened. "Nice to see you are feeling better."

"Why? Because I'm angry?" She shot him a dark look. Marshal had been through so much already. He didn't need these guys poking into his life too.

"Get angry," he said seriously. "Being angry is the best way to avoid becoming a victim." She stared at him, and he nodded. "Once you become a victim in your own mind, it's damn hard to get out of that mentality. All kinds of shit happens in life, but, if it continues to happen, there's no way to stop it. What you need is to ensure that it doesn't continue."

"I had hoped that this would be over soon and that I could move on."

"Soon," Steven promised. "Very soon."

She stared at him, and he shrugged. She realized that he didn't have any answers, but he was trying to make her feel better. She looked over at her mother, who was sitting nearby, hugging a cup of coffee, watching the two of them. "How are you doing, Mom?" Opal asked, as she walked over and gave her mother a hug.

"Angry that they're looking at Marshal, after everything he's done for us," her mother snapped, shooting Steven a dark look.

"I am too, but I understand it," Opal murmured.

"I do, but, after everything we've been through," Ruby wailed, "Marshal's the only one who's been there for us."

"Believe me. I know that," Steven replied.

"So why are you still looking at him then?" Ruby asked Steven.

"Because we have to," he said simply. "Anything less is not doing our job." At that, her mother pinched her lips together and swept up her coffee cup. Making a grand exit, she stated over her shoulder, "I'll be in my room."

"She really does love Marshal."

"I hear that." Steven studied the empty doorway. "I'm glad for both of them. Still doesn't resolve whether he's guilty or not."

"Are you always this inflexible?"

"When it comes to your life? Yes."

She winced at that. "I guess I asked for that, didn't I?"

He smiled. "I know it seems as if we're being cruel, but don't you want to know for sure?"

"Not really. He is the one who saved my life."

"He is, but didn't you ever wonder how he managed to be there on the spot?"

"I listened to his explanation, and it sounded reasonable. And, besides, if I'm being honest, I'm alive, and it's because of him, so I don't really care."

He studied her face for a long moment and then nodded. "I get that too."

The gentleness of his smile made her sigh.

"You hang on to that, and hopefully one day soon we can walk away from the rest of it."

"Are we going anywhere today?" she asked, a tinge of anxiety in her voice. He shook his head. "No, we aren't," he murmured. "It'll be a standard stay-at-home day."

She frowned, hating the relief washing through her. "How are you supposed to do any research if you're stuck here all day?"

"Not your problem," he pointed out, but his lips twitched.

"Oh, you're sending poor Reyes off to do it all."

He chuckled. "I think *poor Reyes* would be happy to be out doing anything he can, rather than sitting here, doing nothing."

She eyed him sideways. "Oh, ouch, so you're on babysitting duty. Is that a punishment?"

At that, he stared at her, then shook his head. "Oh no, you won't get me angry, although comments like that would normally piss me off. I won't rise to the bait."

She frowned. "What do you think I'm doing?" she challenged.

"You're just testing your wings. You go ahead and test, but, no matter what happens. I'm not getting angry."

"And you won't hit anyone?" She hated that *that* question flew out of her mouth, that such a worry could even exist in her mind. Steven had nothing to do with what happened to her. She didn't fear him, yet knowing that didn't make her fear go away.

"Have you ever known me to hit anybody?" he asked, turning to face her to give her his whole attention.

"No," she groaned, "but now I do sometimes find myself looking at men, wondering if they hit women."

"Those kidnappers weren't men. They were paid thugs, who couldn't care less if you were a dog or a man or a child or anything else. If they were paid to beat you up, they just did it. They didn't require brain cells to do it either."

"And what about mothers? Do they have mothers?"

"Usually any healthy childhood relationship has been so long ago, or was such a bad scenario, that they didn't care to be nice, or they didn't know how. They probably didn't have the kind of successful relationship that they could draw on. Men like that, they lose their souls early on," Steven murmured, "and you won't ever change them."

She sank down beside Steven. "I'm sorry. I know you'd never hit anybody."

"Oh, I would and have in my job, but not someone who didn't deserve it and never a woman or a child or an animal."

She looked at him, then nodded. "Let me change that. You never hit anybody without good cause."

"That's better," he said, with a big smile.

"Do you want breakfast?" She needed something to

change the subject and something to keep her busy. Plus this was something she could do for him.

"I would love breakfast."

"I guess my mom isn't keen on feeding you now."

"No, your mom is a little upset with us."

She nodded. "And I get that, but, at the same time, you are here because she asked you to come."

"And I think it went in a direction she didn't expect," Steven noted.

At that, Opal winced. "I guess. You don't really think when you put these things in motion that it'll be so out of your control."

"No, I don't think anybody ever does, and yet we have to clear away the obvious suspects."

His tone was inflexible, and she realized there was no talking him out of looking at Marshal. But she couldn't leave it alone. "Even though the cops already did?"

"They didn't though. They never cleared Marshal. That's the problem. They're still following Marshal. They still have him on a rope that he can't ever get free from. They *still* think he's involved, so, in a way, they still think he knows something. Or that he's somehow connected, and, at the moment, that he's gotten away with something that they're not happy about."

"Seriously?" She stared at him in shock. "Is Marshal really being followed?"

"He is. Whether he's told you or not, he definitely is being followed. Reyes already confirmed that this morning."

"God." She sat down hard and stared at him.

"So, you also have to wonder, since he's being followed, and since he rescued you, did somebody see him do it?"

Opal felt the color fading from her cheeks. "Are you saying that maybe cops are involved?"

"I'm not saying anything yet," he said flatly. "What I *am* saying is that we're not taking any chances. We'll do what we think we need to do, for whatever reason we think we need to do it."

She winced. "Right, got it. It's your investigation, and I need to stay out."

"No, you can't stay out, and we don't want you to stay out. We just need you to understand that we have to follow whatever direction the facts take us."

"I hope that you clear Marshal soon," she whispered. "It would absolutely destroy my mother if she found out he was involved in any way."

"And you," he stated, his gaze piercing.

"And me," she acknowledged, with a nod. "That's not something I want to deal with." And, with that, she turned and headed toward the stove. "I'm making pancakes."

"Perfect."

She stopped for a moment, turned, and looked at him, "Do you still eat like you used to?"

His lips twisted into a lazy smile. "Yeah, I absolutely do."

"Great. Let's hope that the double recipe will be enough."

"I guess if you aren't eating, it will be," he teased in a cheeky tone.

She looked at him to see if he was serious, only to realize that he absolutely was, and then smiled. "Wow, you really are bringing back memories."

Then she got to work.

AFTER BREAKFAST, AND as soon as he got through the section of work he was on, he was still waiting for Reyes to get back. He texted him for an update. **Hey. Anything?** And got absolutely nothing as a response. He stared at the phone, frowned, and quickly sent a message to Levi. **Haven't heard from Reyes. Have you?**

Levi instantly wrote back. **No, how long since you haven't heard?**

Steven checked his watch and texted back. **Three hours. He went to Marshal's place to check on it.**

I don't like that.

Neither do I, but I'm here guarding her and her mother.

Got it. Give me two.

Steven waited, wondering what his options were. He could take off with Opal, but there was no way he was leaving her or her mother behind. However, there was also no way to continue to hide their location, if they kept coming and going. Then Levi called.

"His phone is not pinging a location."

"I'm heading after him." Steven bolted to his feet.

"I don't want you leaving her there."

"I'll take her and her mother with me."

Levi hesitated.

"Listen. You don't have anybody else here right now," Steven snapped, "and if anything happens to Reyes …"

"He's not a green kid, and he knows exactly what the score is."

"That may be, but that doesn't mean that he hasn't found more trouble than he was expecting."

"How much of that trouble is likely to be from Marshal himself?"

"I don't know," Steven said. Grabbing his jacket, he checked his cell phone and his weapon, walked over and spoke to Opal. "Come on. We're going over to Marshal's house."

She turned and frowned at him. "Why?"

"Because Reyes hasn't checked in," he said shortly. "I can't leave you and your mother here alone."

She stared at him, shook her head. "I don't want to go out there."

"But I can't leave you here," he murmured. At that, her mom came running out. "What's the matter?"

"I haven't heard from Reyes, so I want to go over to Marshal's place and see if they are okay."

She stared at him. "I haven't heard from Marshal either." She quickly checked her phone. "I texted him two hours ago and then again about ten minutes ago, and I haven't heard a thing."

"Even more reason to go."

"I'm coming with you then," Ruby stated.

He hated the idea of taking both women but couldn't rightfully leave either alone.

"That's your choice," Opal told her mom, with a dark frown. "We'll both go or neither of us do."

He glared at both women. "You follow my instructions completely. Understand? This isn't a picnic."

"I know that," Opal agreed, "but we also have to figure out if these men are okay, and we need to do it fast."

And, with that, he loaded them both up into her mother's car, pulled out from the garage, where the vehicle had been parked, and followed their directions to Marshal's place. It was just over a ten-minute drive, before he approached a small brickwork house. When he got there, he saw Marshal's vehicle.

"Okay, nobody is leaving this car until I say so. I'm going to check on them. Both of you stay here."

"If you go in there, you're leaving us exposed on the street," Opal said, extreme nervousness spiking her tone.

He nodded. "Very true, but, if I go in there, and gunmen are inside, then it's already too late for both Marshal and Reyes."

Hearing that, Ruby attempted to get out of vehicle, and Steven felt a terrible sense of urgency.

"Right now, let's stop arguing and just go." Ruby bolted from the car, racing to the front door.

Both women were now nearly in a full-blown panic mode, and Steven grabbed their arms, as they ran for the front door. He stopped them and pinned both against the wall. "Stop. Both of you, stop."

They both stared up at him in shock.

"Not one of you takes another step," he growled. "I have to know that the area is secure. Now promise me that you'll both stay here and that you won't move." When they didn't promise, he gave both of them a shake, and immediately they both cried out, "Promise," almost in unison.

"I mean it. I'll know as soon as I go inside."

"And what if the gunmen are inside waiting for you?"

"Yeah, what if they are? Did you think about that? You're both here, and *you* are who they want," he snapped, "and potentially we've walked into their trap. And now there's no way they don't already know we're here."

Opal looked at him in shock. "Shit," she whispered. "We'll stay here, but please don't be long."

"I won't, but I don't want you coming in after me either."

"What if you don't come back out?" she challenged.

"You get back in your car, and you go straight to the police station. Do you hear me?"

She bit her lip, but she nodded.

"Fine," he growled. "Now, stay." She glared at him, and he shook his head. "No, no arguments." And, with that, he slipped up the front stairs and into the house. He stopped at the entrance and stared around him.

Something was off, but it was hard to say what it was. He took two more steps, then he heard an ever-so-quiet noise. He raced in that direction, his gun drawn, and, sure enough, Reyes was on the floor, blood seeping from a wound on his head.

Steven dropped to the floor behind him. Reyes opened his eyes and saw him, then groaned and whispered, "A complete shit show. They caught us inside the place."

"Marshal?"

"I think they took him with them."

Steven nodded, then asked, "Did you find anything? Any reason to suspect that Marshal's part of it?"

Reyes looked at him, as if trying to think his way through it. His gaze was clear, but his words were slow coming. "I guess that would have made it easy for them to have grabbed him and run, wouldn't it?"

"It sure would have, but believe me. For the women's sake, I don't want him to be involved."

"No, neither do I." Reyes shifted slowly onto one elbow, wincing at the movement. "I didn't find anything initially. When I heard sounds of fighting, I went to check but took a hard blow to the head, and that was it for me." Reyes closed his eyes briefly. "Damn it."

"Take it easy. We'll need to get that head checked out."

"I'm fine," he groaned. "I need to get it together, to get these fuzzy thoughts to clear up."

"We'll have to deal with the women too."

"That's *great*." With Steven's assistance, Reyes made it to the couch, where he collapsed and then asked, "Did you leave them at the house?"

"No, unfortunately they're both out front. Be right back." Steven raced to the front door. He opened it, thankful they were both still there.

At the look on his face, Opal covered her mouth with her hand, staring at him in fear.

"I found Reyes with a head injury," he explained. "I'm not sure where Marshal is."

At that, Ruby looked at Steven in horror and then raced through the house, looking for Marshal. When she came back, she was shaking. "Oh dear God. Please don't let anything happen to him."

Steven shook his head. "If it's the same damn kidnapping scenario, we already know how desperate these guys are." At that, Ruby started to bawl. Steven told them, "I need to get back to the warehouse, but I want to do a quick check on this place first."

The women immediately sat down beside Reyes, as Steven went through the house carefully. There didn't appear to be anything out of place. No safes were open, nothing out of the ordinary. He checked the few things in Marshal's bedroom, but nothing indicated a robbery, and that was frustrating in itself, but Steven also knew that there had been plenty of time for Marshal to set things up any way he wanted to. Still a quick check offered no clues of Marshal's potential involvement nor anything related to the intruders.

Plenty of time for Marshal to determine what would be

safe to leave out and what wouldn't be. Marshal also knew that he would be the prime suspect for everybody. Which is why nobody was necessarily even looking for evidence, except for them.

Steven made his way back to the living room, then helped Reyes to his feet, looked at the two women. "Let's go."

"How will we find Marshal?" both women cried out.

"I'm on it." Steven looked over at Reyes. "You got any information that could help?"

Reyes shook his head, then shuddered in pain. "I don't know. I wasn't given a whole lot of chance."

"Yet they didn't kill you," Steven noted.

Reyes continued. "I didn't see them to even know whether there was one or two men here. For that matter, I can't even confirm that they were men."

"No, and I find that interesting." Of course it also added to the whole question of whether Marshal was guilty or not because killing Reyes would compound the case badly.

With that, Steven got them into the vehicle and drove carefully back to Ruby's safe house, watching for possible tails the whole way. There he unloaded them, set Reyes up with an ice pack, his gun, and a laptop. "I've texted Levi an update. I still think we need to get you checked out at the hospital."

"Not needed," Reyes snapped. "I'm fine. I'll see if I can track the vehicle from city cameras."

"You do that, but I'm guessing they've already gone back to the same warehouse."

At that, Reyes nodded slowly. "I guess, in their small minds, it makes sense, doesn't it?"

"It doesn't make any sense," Opal cried out, from behind them. "Surely they know the warehouse is compromised."

Steven looked over at her and sighed. "It could be compromised, or it could be their home base. Either way, we won't get any answers sitting here." He looked over at Reyes. "You good if I go?"

"Yeah, I'm good. I've got this."

Steven turned to the women. "Nobody comes in or goes out. Do you hear me? I mean absolutely nobody. I don't care if it's your best friend, your brother, your sister, whatever. Nobody comes in or out but me." And, with that, he turned and shut the door, calling out for Opal to lock it behind him. He waited outside until he heard the quiet *click* that confirmed the door was locked. Then he raced to the warehouse.

Chapter 7

O PAL STARED FROM the living room window, hidden ever-so-slightly behind the curtains, so anybody from the streets wouldn't see her, as Steven drove away. The white SUV quickly disappeared from view. A chill wrapped around her, with his absence. She was too damn worried about Marshal's kidnapping event now. Although she knew that everybody still believed it was quite possible that Marshal was involved in her father's dirty-cop shenanigans, she didn't believe any of it. If true, it also meant that Marshal knew what had happened to her and had insider knowledge to make it stop. That was too much for her to believe.

It was devastating to even contemplate that he'd known about her kidnapping and torture, and, even though he'd done what he could to save her, she'd still been beaten, nearly drowned, and sent to hell and back over the whole process. And that was something that she would find very hard to forgive.

Yet who was she to sit here and to stand in judgment if she didn't know what was going on? She needed to know the truth. Frowning, unsettled and wishing to God Reyes hadn't been hurt, she returned to the living room, as she faced Reyes. "Are you sure you don't need medical attention?"

He nodded. "I need some time to heal, but, no, I don't need to see a doctor," he told her calmly.

She didn't hear the anger in his voice any longer. Could he have gotten over the attack that fast? "You seem to be relatively calm about the whole thing."

"I'm not happy to be sucker punched, which makes me wonder if the attacker wasn't already in Marshal's house by chance or—" Then he stopped.

"Or?" she challenged.

"Or if Marshal himself attacked me," he added reluctantly.

She gasped, feeling the same fear gripping her soul. "I really, really don't want it to be him," she muttered, sliding down into the chair across from him. She lowered her voice. "I can't imagine what that would mean in terms of what happened to me."

Reyes nodded ever-so-slowly. "It's hard, but these investigations take time. Otherwise the cops would have solved it already." Reyes gave her a grimace. "Obviously we've upset someone. I'm sorry for the stress to you because of it. However, nothing will change until we get answers."

She nodded. "I get that. I just—the whole thing sucks."

"It sucks even more that you think it is Marshal," her mother said harshly from the doorway between the kitchen and living room. "It can't be him."

"You know that for sure?" Reyes asked, looking over at her.

She nodded. "I know that man. I've known him for a long time."

"You also knew your husband."

She flushed at that. "I get your point, but my husband was somebody who kept to himself. He didn't let anything or anyone near the innermost part of him. From the start, he always had secrets, and, as much as I loved him, I loved the man I thought he was, the man I had hoped he was. I can't say that I loved the man who he turned out to be."

"That was also something you didn't know, and even now you're trying to defend Marshal for the same reason."

"He knew you would accuse him, and I went against his wishes and brought you in anyway," Ruby snapped. "Believe me. I already regret that decision."

Opal's stomach clenched at her mother's antagonistic comment. She might regret her decision, but Opal did not. She needed the truth, regardless of what it was.

Reyes stared at Ruby for a long moment. "Of course we have to consider him. That doesn't mean we aren't looking at everyone else at the same time."

Ruby sniffed the air, as if that were a detail not worth arguing about. "You would charge him if you had the chance. I don't know how to convince you that he's not involved."

"As soon as we get all the answers, then we'll know one way or another," he replied. "I would hate to think that somebody so close to you would have done to your daughter what these men did."

At that, Ruby reached a breaking point, and she sagged into the closest chair. "I couldn't live with it. If he was involved in any way, I couldn't live with it." She cried out, "A betrayal like that, after all the other betrayals we've endured, would be beyond me."

Reyes winced at that. "I know that that's how you feel right now, and again, as I said to Opal, we don't have all the answers yet. To get there, we must consider that, and rule out *all* the possibilities."

"I feel terrible that I brought you in," Ruby murmured, as she stared at him, her eyes brimming with tears. "It's making his life hell."

"Even if we find out the truth?"

"What if it's the truth that I can't stand? You will have ruined my life."

"And is that the most important thing?" Opal called out, staring at her mother in shock. "Would you rather believe lies again? How about finding out who did this to me?"

Her mother winced. "You don't understand. I've loved Marshal forever," she murmured.

At that, Opal frowned at her mother, who was tucking her feet up underneath her, as if stalling while trying to figure out what to say. Had her father known? Had he cried? If he had known, that would have been hell on earth for him. Is that what changed him? What sent him down this path? And then finally, not knowing quite what to do, Opal murmured, her gaze intent on her mother's defeated face, "I presume Dad knew."

"I don't know if he knew or not," Ruby snapped, suddenly switching moods, raising both hands. "Do I want to think about that? No, of course not."

"Isn't it possible?" Opal asked.

"Yes, it's possible."

"Were you ever unfaithful?" Opal asked.

"No!"

"But would Dad care about the finer details? You obviously didn't love him anymore and likely lit up whenever Marshal was around. I doubt he couldn't have noticed," Opal persisted.

"I don't know." Ruby stared off in the distance. "I guess it's possible that he guessed it, but he never brought it up. Then we never talked about our relationship, so why would we talk about the one going on around him? Roscoe did change. Our relationship changed. You have to understand. Your father and Marshal are opposites. One is warm, and the other cold. After years of being ..." Ruby showed her palms, turning to Opal. "You're too young to understand."

Opal snorted. "Seriously? If I was ten, maybe even fifteen, you could say that but not now." She shook her head. "I'm still confused though. Why didn't you just leave Dad? You didn't love him any longer, and you wanted a life with Marshal. It's called *divorce*, and they are very common. So why didn't you just divorce him?"

"Because I didn't have enough money, and I doubted your father would be happy about a divorce and would fight me for every penny. Besides Marshal didn't want to do that to his friend."

At that, there wasn't a whole lot she could say, so Opal stared at her mother, wondering at what else she knew and didn't really want to explain. Money and friendship. Yet Marshal had essentially been betraying his best friend if they loved each other anyway. ... Opal was sure her father would have known. Felt it at least.

Her mother was wrong. Her father wasn't cold. Opal had great memories of his easy laughter and his cuddles on the couch, the fun camping trips, and him helping Opal on her school projects. More warm memories than she had of her mother. Her mother was more an indoor *keep the place perfect* type of person. Maybe the two of them had been opposites in the beginning but maybe thought it could work. Obviously over time things had changed. Opal put her money on the divergent pathway as a direct result of the state of this marriage. Too bad Dad wasn't around to ask. And who was Opal to judge? Opal hadn't lived their marriage; she'd been a spectator. Besides, how well did anyone know anyone else?

"So, maybe you know more than you think," Opal murmured.

Her mother looked at her sharply, then shook her head. "If you think I know anything about this, you're wrong. I would never have condoned any action that put you in danger."

Her mother's voice held shock but also something else. Something Opal couldn't put her finger on. The trouble was, Opal found it getting harder to believe her mother, after hearing more about her and Marshal's relationship. Opal was desperate to believe her, but, at the same time, how could she, after just finding out that her mother and Marshal were an item and had been for a long time. Maybe not lovers, but sex was not the definition of a relationship. Or was all this suspicion making Opal crazy? She didn't want to go down that pathway either; she'd been through enough. She needed both Marshal and her mother to be on her side. "Do you think it's why Dad left? Do you think it's why Dad went down his own pathway?" she asked her mother.

"I hope not," Reyes interjected, "but people tend to do things for emotional reasons."

Opal turned and looked at her mother. "Did he have another woman?"

"None that I know of," she said painfully, massaging her temples, "though I would have welcomed it if he did."

"But that's not what I asked," Opal said, striving for calm neutrality. "Because, if he did have somebody else, that would explain some of what was going on here."

Ruby shrugged. "I have no way of knowing. He didn't confide in me."

"No, but was he intimate with you?"

Ruby looked at her, shocked.

Opal shook her head. "Mom, it's well-past time for worrying about discussing this. I don't know whether Dad potentially blamed you for all this or if something else was going on."

"I don't know," she cried out. "If you're asking the last time we made love, I can tell you that it was a very long time ago."

"Right, so he probably had somebody else then." Opal turned and looked at Reyes. "How do we find that out?"

He faced her, a twitch to his lips.

She shrugged. "My father was a strong, virile, and fairly sexual man," she stated. "He attracted women easily. I thought the marriage was sound, but apparently it wasn't. So what are the chances that he had somebody else? Pretty good, I would think. So, if he did have somebody else, are they involved, or are they waiting for him to come set things up so they could move into place? Was he creating a future with someone else? Who knows? And because we don't know, I feel this is something we need to explore." She saw that Reyes agreed with her, but, at the same time, it was something that her mother was really struggling with. She asked her mom, "Did we ever get Dad's cell phone?"

She shook her head. "No, and the cops already looked at his phone records."

"Which wouldn't have had any bearing, if he'd used a burner phone," Reyes murmured.

"Meaning a phone that can't be tracked?" Opal asked.

"Yes."

"He bought them all the time," Ruby said suddenly.

"What do you mean, he bought them all the time?" Opal shrieked.

Ruby shrugged. "He kept telling me that he always needed spare phones for his informants to contact him with, and he would give them out. I never saw any of them. And I did search his desk but found none there."

"Interesting. Any idea where he bought them from?" Reyes asked Ruby.

"No, and the cops came and took everything. My husband confessed to a lot of things, but he never really opened up about having another person in his life."

"Maybe," Reyes suggested, "because he knew that that was something which could no longer go forward, and he didn't want to ruin everybody's life involved."

"Maybe." Ruby snorted. "Seems a little late for that."

"You were also concealing relationships," Reyes noted.

Ruby nodded. "Yes. I have to deal with the guilt of that too."

Reyes nodded as well. "You do because that could have been part of Roscoe's motivation, especially after the department demoted him, while investigating prior allegations. Roscoe would see that as a betrayal at home and at work."

Ruby got up and walked out of the room.

Opal winced. "How long will Steven be?" she asked, staring out the window.

"As long as he needs to be," Reyes reaffirmed immediately.

"Do you think in your heart of hearts that Marshal is involved?" Opal asked Reyes.

"No." Reyes shook his head and winced at the pain. "I would like to think he's not. Still, I can't yet rule him out, and, until I can do that, he remains high on my suspect list."

"Right," Opal murmured.

"I wouldn't worry about that part right now," Reyes murmured. "It's a big thing for you, but, for now, it goes nowhere."

"Yeah, as you said, it is a big thing for me, and it's not exactly something I can turn on and off."

"Of course not," he murmured. "At the same time, you can choose to press the Stop button on your thoughts and to push certain ones off to the side, until we know more."

She frowned at him. "Does that really work for you?"

"Sometimes." He grinned. "An awful lot in my life I've had to push back to try not to let life overwhelm me. Sometimes it works, and sometimes it doesn't, but the more you do it, the easier it becomes."

"I'll take that under advisement," she muttered.

At that, he burst out laughing.

She smiled. "It's nice to hear laughter for a change. It seems—for days, for weeks, for months—all I've heard were tears."

"And while your mother is not here"—Reyes leaned forward and looked at her intently—"I'll be blunt and ask you something."

She winced at that. "You mean about her relationship with my Dad and with Marshal?"

He nodded.

"I don't live at home, haven't for a long time, so, for me, it's a little hard to know if she's telling the truth or not. I want to believe she's telling the truth, but can I? I can't answer that. Right now everything is confusing."

"Fine. You might want to also consider the more that she lies, the worse it looks."

"For Marshal or for her?"

He smiled. "Honestly, for both of them."

"That's not what I wanted to hear."

"Of course not, but this isn't a game that we can play any longer. If your mother knows anything, we need to know it."

"I can try to talk to her again." Opal glanced toward the kitchen. "But, as you can see, she's not very forthcoming."

"And I think that's because she's trying to protect Marshal. But, in protecting him, she could make him look guiltier."

"In other words, you want me to talk to her to see if there's anything she can remember or can think about that would help us." She spread her hands. "I'm sure she's already done that."

"I'm sure she has too," he agreed. "I'm just not sure that what she is remembering is necessarily what we need her to remember."

"How is she supposed to fix that?" Opal asked, surprised.

"Start with her conversations with Roscoe, her discussions about him, anything and everything. Anything that might pertain to what's going on."

At that, she shook her head. "You have no idea what you're asking. The cops have been very insistent all these years since my dad's fiasco started. They didn't give us a break at all. They suspected her. They suspected me. We went under their microscope, and they tore our lives apart. I really can't imagine that anything is left to be found."

"Yet I'm not seeing any of the results of that investigation," Reyes shared.

"Meaning?"

"Meaning that the file is not accessible through the regular channels. Either it's being kept very private, or it's gone missing …"

She wasn't sure how that even pertained to this. Was it possible the investigation file into her father could be missing? As in someone deleted it?

"It's curious," Reyes stated, then frowned. "Either, to the police, this is an ongoing investigation, and nobody gets access yet because they haven't sorted it out themselves, or somebody is keeping it secret and doing the investigation on the side, until the results are brought out." He studied her face and added, "The question is why?"

STEVEN DROVE TO the warehouse, where Opal had been taken as a captive, and parked out of sight on the opposite side of the street. If they had decent cameras up, the kidnappers already knew Steven was here. He hoped that nobody was watching the cameras and that they were more for the warehouse's security, not for the guys using it for whatever purposes they had going on right now.

With a weapon at the ready, Steven quickly slipped over to the building and circled around, looking for a way in, any sign that somebody was inside.

It was quiet, too quiet. That bothered him more than anything because this was his best option for where to look for Marshal, at least until Ice could access the street cameras around Marshal's place or the satellite feed. Hell, even then it would be damn hard to find them. That didn't bode well for Marshal, if he wasn't working with these goons. Time was of the essence, especially considering how quickly these guys had deep-sixed Opal, once they'd picked her up. That still made Steven's blood boil and sent a streak of fear through his guts.

Steven didn't know what the hell was going on, or what they would want with Marshal at this point, but Steven figured it was the same damn thing they had wanted from Opal, information on the stash. But, if so, then they could have collected it from Marshal at any time, so why wait until now?

The only thing that had changed? Well, ... not counting Roscoe's death, two things had changed since then. One, he and Reyes were here. And, two, Opal had survived. If they knew that Marshal had anything to do with her rescue, that would definitely put a nail in his coffin. Unless it was all part of an extended ploy. And because of just how convoluted this could get, Steven wasn't prepared to write off Marshal as a suspect.

In too many ways Marshal looked good for this. Marshal was hiding something. But what? Maybe he was looking into his partner's crimes himself, or maybe he was hoping to find Roscoe's stash. But Steven had a sense that something was going on with Marshal that he wasn't prepared to share. And, of course, as soon as that came up, suspicions were everywhere.

Steven came up to one window, his ears against the wall, listening for any sign of another presence. And then finally he heard it. A voice, indistinct enough that he couldn't really hear what was being said. He slipped along the outside wall, until finally he heard the spoken words.

"Now I've got him," the man shouted, then paused. "Yeah, yeah, yeah. ... No, I don't know what the fuck he knows. I don't know what the hell's going on here. I don't even know why we're back to this. ... We need to just walk away. This one'll take us down, if we aren't careful."

Steven considered that he was just hearing one side of a

telephone call. Still didn't tell him how many were inside.

"A lot of money is involved, and nobody knows where it is. I get that," the man snapped, "but we can't spend it if we're dead. Or in prison. ... Fuck. Even your connections won't keep us out of there. Not at this point. Too many people are involved now, and I don't know who the guys are who I saw at his place. ... There was one, and then I saw the second one come and rescue him, right when I came back. I could only take out one at a time and deal with Marshal too. So I went back and decided I should shoot him, but his partner was there. Who the hell are these guys?"

Steven heard the guy on the phone pacing about inside the warehouse. So Steven had been seen. And this guy had knocked out Reyes, then had kidnapped Marshall. Thank God that Steven had found Reyes when he had, or his partner would be dead. Also now they could absolve Marshal of potentially knocking out Reyes.

"Anybody here that we don't know about is just plain bad news. And I've had a stomach full of bad news at this point," yelled the man, as he continued his rant. "I don't want anything else to do with this mess. ... Yeah, I get it. It doesn't matter what I want," he repeated, with a sneer.

Steven listened to the rest of this guy's end of the phone call, but nothing was helpful, except for the fact that they were after exactly what Steven had suspected, more information. As he peered through the window, he noted one man storming around a small room, with Marshal tied to a chair, seemingly unconscious.

The unconscious part would be a problem, since Marshal wasn't a small man. It would be better if he was on his own two feet, but, if that wasn't an option, then it would be what it was. Steven made his way around the warehouse to every door, trying to find his way in. The last one was unlocked.

He slipped inside and headed for the room where he'd seen Marshal. The room was quiet. Had the guard heard him? Or was he still on his phone call, but listening? Of course Marshal could easily be listening as well—particularly if he was only pretending to be out cold.

Finally the other man broke his silence. "What the fuck? I thought you said somebody was coming."

Steven heard another voice, but he couldn't tell if it was on the phone or if maybe it was Marshal talking. Could be the guy on the other end was just yelling.

"Yeah, yeah, yeah, whatever. I'm not waiting for the boss anymore. I want the information now. I don't have time for this shit. Give it to me, or I'll pop you one. I really don't give a fuck what you want to do."

At that, Steven heard raised voices.

"I don't care. I really don't care. I don't know what the hell's going on. I just want to get out of Dodge, and I want to get out of here now, before I get caught."

Steven slipped up to the doorway, where he could take a look inside the room. Marshal remained tied up and appeared to still be unconscious, while the other man paced, as he spoke on his cell phone again.

"No, he's unconscious. I can't damn well do anything about it, not until he wakes up. I've been waiting on him all this time. ... I've tried water. I've tried everything. ... Yeah, he's an old man. For all I know, I did some serious damage when I knocked him out. And I can't even find the energy to give a shit right now."

Steven watched as the kidnapper tossed down his phone and glared at Marshal. The kidnapper grabbed Marshal's head, pulled it back, and hit him a couple times. But Marshal, whether he was really out or was really good at playing possum, didn't react. And that was hard to do, if you were really awake. Steven watched and waited, while the guy dropped Marshal's head again and started swearing.

"What the fuck!" He looked over at the old man in disgust. "You old fucker, if it wasn't for the fact that they were so sure that you knew something, I'd shoot you right now and make sure you never woke up."

At that, Steven stepped through the door and yelled, "Hands up."

Without warning, the kidnapper turned and fired from the hip. But Steven was no longer in the open doorway; he'd ducked behind the wall.

The kidnapper came running. "No, fucking way," he yelled. "No way are you taking me out right now. I've got too much to live for. I'll take this fucker out first."

"But if you let him die and if that information dies with him, then you know exactly who'll be pissed at you. You ready to take that chance?"

There was a surprised moment of silence on the other side of the wall. "Who the hell are you?" the kidnapper called out.

"Somebody who's looking for the same damn thing."

"What the fuck? You mean we have competition now too?"

"Did you really think that kind of money would go unnoticed?"

"Damn it. … Look. I don't want the money. I just want to get out of here."

"Yeah, that's nice, but you're the one who's sitting there with a prisoner I want."

"I don't give a shit what you want. If I don't get the information, I'm already in trouble."

"You're in trouble *now*," Steven declared. "Maybe you want to rethink your position and run out that window and disappear."

"Yeah, as if you'll let that happen. And, if the guys find out what I did, my life isn't worth anything."

"Your life isn't worth anything anyway," Steven called out. "You already know it. You're nothing but a henchman who's already failed because you didn't get the other guy. You should have popped him."

An ugly silence followed on the other side. "Are you here to take me out? Is that what you're fucking doing there? Taking me out now? How is that even fair? I did everything they asked. Why the hell are you here?"

"You might be surprised."

"I doubt it." But such bitterness filled his voice, that Steven wasn't surprised at what the kidnapper did next. He fired at the open doorway.

"Wow, that was really effective." Steven laughed. "How much ammo have you got left now?"

But the man wasn't done swearing, and the blue streak continued, as he lost his temper, and then his fear took over. "God damn it. I don't have enough money to leave."

"Yeah, you do. It's amazing how many people say that, when they really don't have a clue how little they need." Steven didn't want to shoot this guy, but it would be best if he could turn him to help them. Yet this kidnapper's life would be over for sure.

"Yeah, broke is not exactly the way I wanted to leave."

"Of course not, you want to go out in a blaze of glory, knowing that you hit the big paycheck. Haven't you figured out that the big paychecks never get paid? All that ends up happening is that guys like you get put down so those big paychecks don't have to be paid at all."

After a short hesitation, the kidnapper gave an ugly laugh. "I was afraid of that, but, no, I convinced myself that I would be too useful and that nobody would take me out."

"Yeah, how do you feel about it now?" Steven didn't know how far he could push this guy, but he also knew that he needed him out of bullets or to leave Marshal alive long enough for Steven to get in there and to get Marshal out. When Steven heard no sounds for at least ten seconds, Steven started to get worried. "What's the matter, rethinking your position?"

He heard an odd sound, unsure of exactly what it was, yet it sent him to the edge, waiting for the attack to come. When it didn't, he waited longer, wondering what was going on.

Finally another voice called out, "He's gone."

At that, Steven poked his head around the corner, and, sure enough, the gunman had bolted out the window. He looked over at Marshal, who sat upright in the chair, staring at him. His face was banged up, but otherwise he looked okay.

"I'm surprised he left you alive."

"I think he decided that a few minutes extra would make the difference to his getaway."

"Probably would have, but we'll find him anyway."

At that, Marshal gave Steven a half smile. "You want to get me out of this?"

"Yeah," he said, as he walked over. He holstered his gun, then quickly freed him. "How's the head?"

"Harder than normal," Marshal quipped. "I'll be fine."

He got up, slowly stretched, and groaned. "But I really would like to get the hell out of here."

"Yeah, you and me both. Interesting that they used the same location."

"Is that where we are?" He stared around in surprise. "Yeah, it is, damn. They really are creatures of habit, aren't they?"

"I think maybe they found a place that worked and don't know where else they can go."

"That's possible too," he muttered. "Asshole," he added, staring out the window.

"Yeah, but that asshole is long gone, and we need to be too."

As Steven walked Marshal back out to the car, Steven studied the older man. He walked fine, straight, without assistance. His face had taken the worst of it. "Do you need medical attention?"

"No, I'm pissed, sour, and angry, but alive, so I'm fine."

As Steven started the engine, he said, "Let's get you home. If nothing else, you'll need time to recover."

"I don't want to recover," he snapped. "I want to go for the jugular."

"If you point us in the direction of a jugular, we can go after it. That would be great. In the meantime, it'll be a recovery period for you."

He groaned. "Damn it. You know what the women will say when I get home."

"Yeah, they'll call you an old man, say you're too old to do the job, and that you need to stay home and look after them."

He snorted at that. "*Women*."

"Yep, can't live with them, can't live without them."

Steven laughed. "But that is what they'll say." Sure enough, by the time he got Marshal inside, and the women were all over him, it was obvious that he wouldn't go anywhere for a while.

Marshal looked over at Steven. "You could get me out of this."

"Nope." Steven grinned. "I'm not getting you out of anywhere. I've done my job. Now you need to stay inside and stay safe for a bit, and you definitely can't go back to your place."

"Yeah, I got that. Damn it to hell anyway."

"Yeah, did you recognize the guy at all?"

"No, I didn't, and I didn't hear most of the conversations. I only came to when he started firing. Came to with a shock to see that he was so pissed off."

"I tend to have that effect on people. It's handy though," Steven said, looking over at Marshal.

"Thanks," Marshal said gruffly to Steven, his arm around Ruby.

"Yeah, you're welcome," Steven replied. "Make sure I don't regret it."

At that, he didn't say anything at first but nodded. "I'm not the bad guy here."

"That would sure be nice to confirm," Steven muttered. "The women are certainly on your side."

He smiled. "We've been close these last few years," he admitted. "I wouldn't do anything to ruin that."

"I'm glad to hear that because they've been through enough already."

"Agreed." With that, Ruby enveloped him in a hug and held him close. When Marshal finally stepped back, he looked at her, brushed the hair off her face. "I've brought it up before, and I'll bring it up again, but I think, by the time this is over, we should leave this neck of the woods."

She nodded immediately. "I don't know where you want to go, but I'll have to sell the house first."

"We can put that in the hands of a Realtor," he said immediately. "I just want to get the hell away from all this. I have to get away from all the people who obviously think I know something, and of course I don't." He growled in frustration. "Nobody ever believes me."

"They aren't wrong," Reyes pointed out. "Roscoe was your partner, and, as far as they're concerned, you might very well have been a major part of whatever is going on," Reyes murmured from the couch.

"And there's nothing I can do to convince anybody that I'm not part of it," he muttered.

"That's because it doesn't make sense."

"It makes a whole lot of sense if you're me." Marshal twisted to glare at Reyes. "All I gave a shit about was Ruby here. I didn't care about my partner. He became a wild card, and I was trying to figure out what the hell was going on and how I could get him to let her go, so we could have a future together. But you can bet that that wasn't something that I could get from him easily. I even started investigating him myself, trying to figure out what the hell was going on. I followed him quite a few times to see who he was meeting on his jaunts. And I never saw anything. That pisses me off more than anything because it means he knew that I was following him, and he had successfully avoided me."

"Or to keep you guessing," Steven suggested, with a nod. "The fact that he would even go to those kinds of lengths says a lot."

"Believe me. I know, and I feel like an ass because I

couldn't figure it out," he muttered.

"It's not your fault." Ruby patted his chest reassuringly. "I didn't know either."

"That's because you weren't looking," Opal said. "Like him, you were only concerned about moving on, but you didn't want to just ask him for a divorce, and I'm still not too sure why."

"Because he was getting quite unpredictable," Ruby said, "and I hate to say it, but I was getting afraid of him. I was afraid of what he would do if he found out who I wanted to be with."

"Of course because that's another huge betrayal, isn't it?" Opal stated.

"Yes, of course it is," Ruby cried out painfully, "but what were we supposed to do? I was very unhappy, and I wanted out, but getting out wasn't something I could just turn around and do." She glared at her daughter. "I know that you seem to think you know everything, but you don't. You don't know what it was like with him the last few years. He was different."

At that, Opal sighed, sat in the nearest chair, and nodded.

Steven walked over, sat down beside her. "Hey, how're you doing?"

"I'm okay. It's been a rough day. Another rough day in a long line of rough days." She gave him a wan smile. "I hate to admit it, but I'm feeling pretty exhausted again."

Chapter 8

O PAL WOKE UP from her nap, unsurprised to find that she was still tucked up against Steven's shoulder. She gently patted his chest, snuggled closer, and yawned. "This is becoming a bad habit."

"I think it's a good habit," he murmured, wrapping an arm around her and holding her carefully. "Obviously it's what you need to be able to sleep."

"Sure, but for how long?" she asked. "I'm not used to depending on someone for something so simple as sleep."

"Doesn't matter," he countered. "This is not the time to be worried about such things."

She knew he was right. "It definitely isn't, but it's hard not to." Yet he made it all sound so sensible and so normal, and yet none of it was. Nothing about any of this could be labeled *normal*. And yet she could do nothing to make it that way either. She yawned and gave him a hug and then slowly shifted, wincing as her back complained from her awkward sleeping position.

"Sore?" he asked.

"All of me is sore still."

He nodded. "It'll take several more weeks. You know that, right? Soft tissue damage takes a while to heal."

"I was hoping it would take less," she mumbled. "My face is still hot and swollen. Everything feels as if I've been run over by heavy machinery."

He smiled. "You have been, so honor the healing process. Try not to get too far ahead of yourself and all this." Steven waved his hand around the room. "Realize and accept that it will take time to get where you want to be."

"Taking time is one thing," she muttered. "I don't want it to take more time than it needs to."

He chuckled. "I was expecting you to not be very tolerant anyway, so this attitude isn't really a surprise."

She looked at him, then shrugged. "I don't have patience for being ill."

"You never did, as I recall."

"I never understood that," her mother spoke up from within the circle of Marshal's arms. "I don't know how it is that you could possibly not go down sick like the rest of us," Ruby said peevishly. "It's almost as if you have some extra healing ability. Even if everyone else was sick, you were fine."

"Oh, if I were to have such a talent, I could really use it right now." She yawned again.

"Do you want to go back to sleep?" Steven asked her.

"No, now that everybody's home, safe and sound, I guess I could use some food."

"Such a mundane thing," her mom noted. "I don't even think I can cook right now," she cried out, her arms shaking and wrapping around her own body. "I need this all to go away."

"Which is also why I'm suggesting we leave," Marshal reminded her, his voice only off a little from his recent attack.

Opal could sympathize. "I don't want to run. I want this over. I want it finished, and I want closure. But this is my hometown. There's no reason I should have to leave. I didn't do anything wrong."

"Maybe," Steven pointed out, "but that doesn't mean that, as far as the rest of the world is concerned, you can have that same peace and quiet just yet."

"What will it take?" she asked.

"Finding out whatever the stash is and making it public, so nobody has any cause to continue to look for it. Plus taking down anybody we find along the way who is looking for it."

She hesitated. "I don't even know what you're talking about for a stash."

"He said cash. But I can't tell you that's it for sure," Steven offered. "It could be online. It could be something tangible, like drugs. It could be a USB key. It could be more than that."

"If it's a USB key, then check with the cops," Ruby suggested. "They took everything."

"Not everything." Opal stared at her mom.

"Yes, they took everything," Ruby snapped, raising her hands. "Sure they brought a lot of it back. They had to, particularly after Roscoe died. And, speaking of the dead, I still have to make arrangements." She scrubbed her hands on her face. "I'll go to my room and see if I can make some of these decisions, so I can get something off my plate." Obviously upset, Ruby turned and headed into another room.

Opal looked over at Steven. "I wonder if I should go to her."

"If you want to. Decisions have to be made about your father's funeral, right?"

"I think he should just be cremated. Nice, simple, and effective."

"She doesn't?"

"I think she agrees, but I think she also feels guilty because she just wants it all to end, and it won't be so simple."

"Of course it won't, but if you don't make decisions ..."

"I know. Let me go talk to her." And, with that, Opal got up and followed her mom into the office. There her mother sat at the desk, staring down at its top.

"Let's set up a cremation," Opal suggested.

"Do I have to pick up the ashes too?" she asked bitterly. "I don't want anything to do with him."

"I get it, but I don't think that's an option. We are his kin, and we do have to deal with it."

"*Right*," Ruby muttered.

Opal nodded. "Then we can throw his ashes out in the wind somewhere, take a drive, since he always wanted to go back to nature."

Her mother snorted at that. "Who the hell knows what he wanted? And why should I care?"

"He didn't tell us anything differently, I don't think." And then she looked at the room. "What about his will?" she asked, looking blankly at her mom. "Do you have it? His wishes should be there."

"I don't even know what will?"

"Oh my God." Opal sat down on a spare chair, staring at her mother. "Did you contact the lawyer?"

She immediately shook her head. "No, I didn't even think about it."

"Do you even know if his will is valid anymore?"

"No, I don't know anything. Your father handled all that stuff."

With a wince, Opal picked up her father's stack of business cards, pulled out the one that she knew belonged to the lawyer—or at least the lawyer she knew of last—and made a phone call. When she identified herself, he immediately became friendlier on the other end.

"Hey, how are you doing?"

"It's been a shit show," Opal admitted. "I presume you heard the news."

"I did, yes, and I've been expecting your call. I'm surprised it took you this long."

"My mother wasn't exactly sure if you were even the lawyer anymore."

"Yeah, I've still been handling your father's business affairs."

"So, do you know anything about his will? Is there anything in there that we're expected to do?"

"If you don't want to do anything," he said all business-like, "I can handle it."

"My mother would certainly appreciate that," Opal noted. "I'm not sure, but I need to know. Am I part of the will? Is my mother? Do we need to do anything? Does it contain his wishes for a funeral? I feel completely in the dark right now."

"I did take a look at the will, and you are mentioned. I can send you a copy. And there is a bequest he's made for you. And I have it here."

"Fine." Opal winced at the look her mother shot her, like sharp daggers. "Is there any mention of my mother?"

"Not now," he said, with an apologetic note. "Not since he went to jail. He changed his will at the time."

"Or at least once she filed for divorce, I suppose," she added.

"He didn't have any worldly goods left anymore at that point in time. Everything was pretty well taken for the lawsuits. The house is still a sticking point, and I do need to speak to your mother about that. It's in both their names, but, as he's passed on, it's hers. However, there is a hold on it due to his debts."

"Right," she whispered, with a headshake, knowing this would be a blow to her mother. "That's why I'm surprised to hear he had anything left."

"He didn't leave much, just a small package for you."

"Fine, I'll come down and get it." Then she stopped. "Or can you courier it to me?"

"Is the media still hounding you?" he asked in sympathy.

"Yeah, you could say that," she muttered, thinking of her face. The last thing she wanted was questions, and she wasn't supposed to have any contact with the outside world. She realized as soon as she had that thought that the men would be pissed at her. "Look. Let me call you back, and I'll figure out what I can do."

"Sure enough," he said. "Call me back."

She hung up, raced to the other room, her mother following her, and cried out, "I screwed up."

Both men looked at her. "What do you mean?" Steven asked.

"I phoned the lawyer, to sort out my dad's funeral arrangements, and he has the latest will."

They stared at her. "And?"

"Apparently my father left me a small package." She raised both hands in frustration.

"Okay." The two men looked at each other, as if trying to process how much damage she'd done.

Steven looked at Ruby, then Marshal. "I thought you had the will? He had another one?"

Ruby nodded, her voice harsh as she glared at him. "So

did I, but apparently he wrote a new one." Her gaze locked with Marshal's.

"I contacted the lawyer." Opal tried to keep her voice reasonably calm. "Regarding the funeral arrangements and anything else I needed to know about, and he told me that Dad had changed his while he was in jail. You told me not to have any contact, but my mother didn't want to deal with the funeral. Honestly, I didn't even think about not calling the lawyer. I knew it needed to be dealt with. So I grabbed the phone and called him."

"What else did he say?"

"He said that he could deal with the funeral arrangements, as per the will," she said, "and I feel that's probably a better idea for my mother."

"That's a good idea," Steven agreed, "but, if something from your father is there, you need to go and collect it."

"I don't really want him to see my face," she admitted, "so I asked if he could maybe send it by courier."

"Right, was your mother incapable of making that phone call?" Reyes asked.

She winced, looked back at the office, and shrugged. Her mother and Marshal had walked out of the living room, leaving her on her own. "I'm really not sure about that. At the moment, she seems as if she's falling apart more."

The two men stared at her for a long moment and then nodded.

She lowered her voice. "There's nothing for my mother, and Dad had nothing left." She then explained about the house and the lien against it.

"Ouch." Steven stared at the empty doorway, obviously deep in thought. "Let me see what I can make happen with the package. I don't want you to go out in public right now."

"I really don't want to either. I wasn't supposed to let anyone know I'm alive as it is."

STEVEN UNDERSTOOD WHY she'd done it, but it was frustrating. He got up, walked over, wrapped her up in his arms. "We'll deal with it. I did question your mother about the will. It never occurred to me that the lawyer would have an updated copy, and that's on me."

"We'll deal with it," she whispered back to him, "but it's not something we should have to deal with. We already have so much to deal with. And I couldn't take it anymore. I needed to have something resolved."

"Do you want the lawyer to handle it, or do you want us to handle it?"

"He's still my father," she said painfully. "I want to get his body cremated and maybe take a walk somewhere and dispose of his ashes, wherever I'm allowed to do so."

"Let me contact the lawyer, and I'll set it up."

She looked at Steven gratefully. "Are you sure?"

"Of course I'm sure, but I don't want you going there alone, and I don't want you facing him alone."

"I'll just as soon not face him at all," she muttered.

"Now that might not be a choice," Steven noted. With that, he took her phone, hit Redial, and, when the lawyer answered, he identified himself. "We're trying to figure out how to get the package that he left, and we will take care of the burial as per the will, providing it's something simple, like cremation."

"He did want to be cremated," the lawyer confirmed, "and his ashes dropped off the bridge into the river. But that's no longer legal. So something along the line would be fine. I did tell him at the time, but he didn't particularly care."

"That we can manage," Steven told him, "if for no other reason than Opal needs the closure."

"I get that," the attorney said. "She's been through hell and back."

"She has, indeed." He glanced at Opal. "Now do we have to come in person and see you?"

"In this case, I think it would be better, since I need to know for sure that she's getting this package herself."

Steven hesitated and then asked, "Any chance of a house visit? She's been quite sick."

"Oh." The attorney hesitated. "I could stop on my way home from work maybe," he said cautiously. "She hasn't got anything contagious, does she?"

"No, nothing contagious. That would be good if you could come by," Steven murmured. "She's also staying at another place because of the media." Opal gave him the address.

"Fine. I'll see if I can do it today then. I'll call you when I'm outside, so you know it's me."

And, with that, Steven disconnected and looked over at her. "Does that work? As much as I hate to give your location, I didn't want to take you out in public. But," he warned, "this could mean moving again for safety."

"It works fine." She sniffled back a tear.

He grabbed her hand. "Hey, it's one thing you can do to help him and to finish this. I do understand that he's still your father."

"That's the thing. My mother is quite angry about it. And now more so."

"Angry that you want to dispose of his ashes?"

"Angry that I want anything to do with him," she whispered. "And I understand. I really do. She was put through hell and back over all this, but I just …"

"Stop, Opal. You don't have to make excuses. You don't have to try to get anybody to understand. This is still your father. You still need to say goodbye, if for no other reason than so you can move on."

She nodded. "Thank you. It figures that you would understand."

"The world's too small, too convoluted, and too full of pain to not understand." He stroked her swollen cheek gently. "Your mother will come to that point herself."

"Maybe," Opal muttered. "It's hard because I feel as if she and I are drifting apart, all because of my father."

"You don't have to."

"No, but, at the same time, it's happening anyway." He nodded and didn't add to it. Finally she looked over at him. "It's only a few hours until the lawyer is here, so I need food, maybe a shower. Now that Marshal's safe, I need to recover a little bit."

"You need to disconnect," Steven suggested, with a smile. "Can you put on a movie, or do something that would help take some of this out of your brain?"

"I don't know. With Marshal being kidnapped like that, it just brought right back to the forefront everything about my own kidnapping. I feel like butter scraped across toast, raw inside."

"That's to be expected," Steven told her, "and that's why it's even more important to find a way to disconnect from all of it."

"That sounds so simple," she cried out, "but it's almost impossible. Every time I close my eyes, there are these memories."

"And they'll be there for a while. Unfortunately, although you were doing better, Marshal's kidnapping has set you back again. But that's to be expected. Now, dealing with the lawyer, your father's will, will also trigger more emotions and upset."

She nodded slowly. "It really did, and that makes me angry because I thought I was doing so well."

"You were, and you will be again." She stared at him distrustfully, and he smiled. "I haven't lied to you."

"No, you haven't lied to me." Then she gave him a half smile. "But I'm not exactly sure that you've been fully honest."

"I have been," he protested, opening his arms wide in a show of innocence.

She shrugged. "Maybe I'm not even ready to hear all the truth right now. Yet it seems as if there are undercurrents going on here."

"Definitely. I'm glad you noticed, and I was going to ask you about them."

"I don't even know what to say," she muttered, "because I don't understand them."

"And that brings me back to one of the questions I asked you earlier." She shuddered and refused to respond. He opened his arms, and she stepped into them.

"Please, no," she whispered, and he held her close.

He could hope it was a no, and he also knew that the crux of the matter would happen much faster. He didn't know if it would blow apart, and would he probably get the answers he needed, or would it be something where they'll only get partial answers? He hoped, for her sake, it would be complete, but no way to know yet. "Let's wait and see what the lawyer has for you," he muttered.

"Why would my father give me anything?" she asked bitterly. "He hardly saw me these last few years."

"Did you have words with him?"

"Lots of words. I went to the jail to see him," she shared. "I wanted to know if he really had done all that. He never said anything. He just looked at me with a slight smile. Didn't say yes. Didn't say no. Finally I ended up walking out. I found it a very difficult visit," she muttered.

Steven turned her around and led her to the kitchen. "Remember that food part," he muttered.

"Yeah, is that your answer for everything?"

"No, but, hey, it might work for right now. While your mind is chewing away on all those memories that hurt, your stomach acids are being pumped out in a way that'll destroy your system. So let's get some food in there and see if we can make it a bit easier on you."

"Maybe," she muttered, "but how do I even eat with all this going on?"

"You eat because, without it, you aren't in a position to deal with anything," Steven replied. "It's way too important to have your system functioning at peak performance, just in case."

"What? Just in case I get kidnapped again?" She shuddered in place. "God, I'm sorry. Just when I think that I'm holding it together, something happens, and I realize I haven't gotten anything together at all."

"And who said you have to be perfect?" he murmured, holding her hand. "I personally like you just the way you are." It broke Steven's heart to see Opal fight and struggle so much, but it was to be expected, and it was a horror that would live with her forever. The only thing he could say was that time would diminish its effect on her, once she realized she was safe.

But that couldn't happen now because, at the moment, particularly with the kidnapping of Marshal, Opal knew that she wasn't safe and that the threat was still out there, hovering at the edge of her consciousness. Maybe if Marshal himself hadn't gotten kidnapped, things would be better for her. Right now, however, absolutely no way for her to see a path forward that didn't seem to be bad news forever.

Steven knew it would get better. He knew that there would be progress on the case, one way or the other, but he couldn't guarantee that her sense of relaxed confidence would ever return or that there would be a peaceful existence ahead for her. Not anytime soon.

How had anyone known where to grab her? Had they followed her? Had they watched her house? Her job? It was easy enough to follow her to work; it was easy enough to even track her phone in this day and age.

The fact that her father had used burner phones all the time was interesting too. And it would have immediately made everybody around him suspicious. Steven hadn't seen any of the case files on the charges against Roscoe or Marshal, and for a moment Steven contemplated a scenario where her father hadn't been guilty, yet had pled guilty for some particular reason, … like to save Opal.

But Steven hadn't been raised to believe in fairy tales either. If Roscoe had confessed, who was Steven to say it was anything other than the truth?"

As they waited for the lawyer to show up, he kept a close eye on Opal, as she busied herself almost frantically in a set of unnecessary tasks. She mixed up a cake and popped it in the oven and then made sandwiches. After the cake was done and cooled, she iced it into a beautiful three-layer cake, which anyone would be proud to serve. He noted the attention and care that she took. Yet it was almost as if it was *too much* focus and care, as if she didn't dare pull her attention away from it for a second, in case she fell apart. And once again he found his own heart bleeding for her.

When he thought it was safe, he asked, "How are you now?"

"I don't know. Honestly, I'm filling time, trying hard not to freak out."

"I get that." He grinned broadly. "Yet we'll all appreciate the cake later on."

She stopped, stared at it, and then chuckled. "I didn't even think about that, but you've always been a chocolate cake person, haven't you?"

He nodded, still smiling. "Yep. I've always been a sweet-tooth guy, although let's not limit me to cake. I do happen to love my cookies too."

"Do you want me to make some?" she asked, her hand automatically reaching for the cookbook beside her.

He shook his head. "No, I don't want you to burn your-self out."

"Burning myself out worrying is one thing, but distract-ing myself by baking cookies is a completely different thing."

"Hey, don't stop her if she wants to," Reyes called out, from the other side of the room. "I love cookies too."

She chuckled. "I have a really good recipe, if you're up for some really big chocolate chip cookies."

"Yeah, that sounds pretty good," Steven replied, with a surprised smile. "But again I don't want you to exhaust yourself."

"I need to be exhausted. Otherwise I won't sleep again,"

she muttered.

There was a lot of truth to that, so he let her go, but he stayed in the kitchen and worked while she baked. She prepared something and then something else, and then something more, sticking each into the oven. He frowned, wondering if he should say something, then decided it was probably better to just let her go. If nothing else, they could always take the extra items to the food bank or just freeze them. He was pretty sure that, with a little help from Reyes, the two of them could do some serious damage to anything she produced.

She had just popped something else into the oven, when the doorbell rang.

Chapter 9

O PAL FROZE, ALMOST in a panic.

Steven immediately got up, walked over to her, and said, "The lawyer, remember? It's just the lawyer. I opened the gate a little bit ago for him."

She took a deep breath. "Right." She lifted a shaky hand to her forehead. "God, I'm such a mess."

"That's not the point. And you look fine," he added. "You'll need to be present."

"If he's worth his salt as an attorney, he should at least verify who I am, before receiving the package," she agreed, with a nod, hating the sweaty palms she couldn't control. Wiping her hands on her pants, she added, "As much as I don't want to go out there and let him see me and the condition I'm in, it is important that I at least let him see me."

"Let's take him to the office."

As she walked to the front door, with Steven close behind, she asked, "Can I open it?"

"He did call ahead, as he told us earlier. However, you don't even have a peephole here, do you?" he asked. "Go to the office. We'll conduct business there." He waited until she stepped back, out of sight but she couldn't not keep her eyes on him. From where she stood, she could just barely see as Steven opened the door to a businessman with a briefcase, looking around nervously. "Hey, I'm Steven. We spoke on the phone. Come in. Thanks for making the trip. Step inside."

The lawyer immediately stepped in and was greeted by Ruby. He stated, "It's so strange to even be here. The last time I was at your home, the media was a nightmare. I can understand why you moved out. But the thought of them finding you here, in this rural setting, would be enough to make anyone want to run away." He returned his gaze to Steven. "I don't know you."

"No, you don't. I'm a friend of the family. And this matter is private," Steven said to the lawyer.

"I'm glad to hear there is still some privacy for them," he said in a sudden abrupt tone. "This family has been through hell."

"Agreed," Steven replied, motioning the lawyer into the hallway, where the lawyer's gaze landed on Opal's face.

The shock of seeing her hit him visibly. "Oh my God," he cried out, dropping the briefcase. "Are you okay?"

"I am now." She smiled. "So maybe you can understand another reason why I didn't want to come to your office."

He was speechless. "My dear, I don't know what happened, but my word …"

When he seemed so completely lost, she took pity on him, walked over, and gave him a gentle hug. "Thank you. It's good to see you. It's been quite a while."

"Yes, it has been quite a long time. You were in high school back then, I believe." He slowly collected his wits. Picking up his briefcase, he shook his head and was quickly shown to the office and sat where indicated. "And yet it's still under terrible circumstances."

"I figured that went along with your job," she noted

teasingly.

He nodded. "There are definitely some aspects of my job that force me to deal with terrible circumstances," he admitted. "In this case, it's not that big of an issue, … as least I didn't think so." He looked around, with a worried expression. "Even that seems very strange to say." He glanced back at Steven. "Are you a bodyguard?"

Steven nodded. "Something like that. The attack on Opal was done before I got to her." He gave the lawyer a quick summary, leaving out most of the details.

"We have no illusions about my father," Opal said bluntly. "We've been to hell and back over his actions."

Ruby remained strangely silent.

The lawyer nodded. "I have to admit I was pretty upset myself. He was a really good friend for a very long time and to find out, … well, you know far better than I could say." Finally he shrugged and didn't add to it, and they all appeared grateful.

Getting down to business, he began, "I only need to speak with Opal, and I have specific instructions to give this to her privately." He looked over at Ruby. "I'm sorry, Ruby."

"It's fine." Ruby shook her head. "I want nothing to do with that man anyway." And, with that, she walked into the kitchen.

Opal called out, "Can you take the cookies out in ten minutes, Mom?"

"Yes, of course."

And, with that, Opal asked anxiously, "Is it okay if Steven is with me? I'm quite paranoid about closed doors these days."

The lawyer nodded in understanding, "Your father didn't say that no one else could be here. Honestly, he didn't want your mother here."

"Fine." She looked over at Steven, who nodded and immediately took his spot beside her.

"How long have you two known each other?" the lawyer asked Steven, possibly seeing the protective manner in which he'd stayed by Opal's side.

"Decades. If I had known she was in trouble earlier, I would have been here a lot sooner."

"Yes, it tends to be that we don't hear of these problems until it's so far down the road that all we're doing is picking up the pieces."

"Exactly," Steven agreed. "So, why don't you go ahead and tell her whatever it is that she needs to know."

"It's not so much that she needs to know anything," he said sadly. "I'm just trying to ensure that I follow things to the letter, so I can discharge my own responsibilities."

She smiled. "So, discharge away. Obviously you can tell this is a bone of contention between me and my mother."

He nodded. "I understand both sides of that. First off, here's a copy of the updated will." He handed her an envelope. "You'll see that your father basically didn't have anything left, just enough to cover his burial costs and my fees. Honestly, if there wasn't enough to cover the fees, I would be totally okay to walk away from that too. As I alluded to earlier, he was a friend of mine, and I, … I don't quite understand what happens to people sometimes."

He watched as she accepted the will, and her words were choked back by tears.

Steven moved closer and slipped an arm around her shoulders for support.

She looked back at him and smiled. "I didn't think it would be this tough."

"All kinds of things in life can be tough. Don't be ashamed of it. Honest emotion is honest emotion."

She nodded. "It's such a weird feeling though."

"Got it," he said gently. "Let's get through this."

And, with that, the lawyer continued. "I don't even need to be here more than another minute." He handed her a small parcel, about the size of a jewelry box. "This is what your father left for you. I don't know if there's an explanation. I don't know if a letter's in there. I don't know anything about it," he said quietly. "It is sealed. I have not seen the contents, and I hope it doesn't upset you terribly."

"Me too," she replied, looking at the attorney wryly. "My father was a man of many surprises. Some good, some bad, and some far worse than I could have imagined."

"But he was still your father."

"Exactly," she murmured. "As far as his body …"

"I can take care of it, if you wish, or you can. I understand you need to find closure in some way as well."

"If you can at least confirm the crematorium and get his ashes, I'll pick them up and dispose of them as he wished in the will, at least as close as I can. And then, like you, I'll feel as if I've discharged my duty."

He nodded. "Fine, I'll call the crematorium and make arrangements for payment. There is money for that in the estate, as specified."

"Perfect." She looked down at the package in her hand and sighed. "I think I'll wait to open this."

"You do it when you want to," he agreed gently. "I don't know anything about it. I'm grateful you have somebody here with you in case it becomes very emotional."

"I'm sure it will be. No way for it to be otherwise."

With that, they walked him back out to the front door.

Outside, he turned to her once more and said, "If you need anything, call me."

She smiled. "Thank you." She watched from the front entrance, hiding behind the curtains, as he got in his vehicle and drove away. As she turned back to the living room, Steven had been standing right beside her the whole time, ever constant with his silent support.

Whereas her mother appeared to be steaming with outrage.

"I still don't understand why you had to accept any responsibility for his funeral." Ruby sniffed, her hands on her hips, her foot tapping the floor, as she glared at Opal.

"No, I understand you don't. However, I need to do what I need to do for my father. To do what feels right for me." On that note she walked back into the kitchen and put another tray of cookies in the oven, without saying another word.

INTERESTED TO SEE what was going on with the mother, Steven sat back ever-so-slightly, so he could hear the muted conversation, as Marshal tried to get Ruby to calm down.

"He did nothing for us," she snapped viciously. "We should have left him to mold in the morgue."

"That's not the answer," Marshal replied. "Let's calm down. It's been a trying day for all of us."

"Maybe, but Opal's already been through enough. Why must she go through this as well?"

"Because she wants to," Marshal said firmly. "We all have to grieve in our own way."

"Well, I'm not grieving," Ruby snapped. "I'm too damn glad that bastard's gone." And, with that, she stormed off.

Steven moved toward the kitchen, acknowledging Marshal with a smile.

"Just like she has to grieve in her way," Marshal said, with a nod toward Opal, who was busy working on the cookies, "so does Ruby, and unfortunately they have very different methods. Anger is very normal."

"It is and it isn't."

"It's hard to watch them suffer so much." Marshal groaned. "At the same time, it feels as if I can't even grieve myself. Even though I have no right to grieve at all."

"You do, but, like everyone, you'll have to do it in your own way."

"And that's hard," he muttered.

Walking into the kitchen, Steven asked Opal, "Will you tell me what your dad gave you?"

"Looks like a jewelry box, but I haven't opened it." He raised one eyebrow, and she shrugged. "I'm not ready to open it."

He nodded slowly. "I get that. I guess that's another thing we all need to do on our own."

She pulled out the cookies, put them onto a cooling rack, and stared down at them for a long time.

He drew her closer and gently held her. "No pressure."

She smiled. "From you, no, but from them? ... I feel pressure. Everybody's curious. Everybody wants to know."

"That doesn't matter," Steven said. "This is your life. You get to do what you want to do, and, for the moment, it doesn't matter about them. It will soon though, as we need to know if it's pertinent to what's going on here."

She looked up at him. "Is it wrong that I feel disconnected, that instead of being closer to my mother, this whole mess has pushed us even further apart?"

"How close were you before?" he asked curiously.

"I thought we were close." Opal shrugged. "But how close can anybody be when a marriage is disintegrating in front of you, and your father is being accused of horrible crimes, and then he pleads guilty, and you realize that your whole life has been a lie? I think that's the part my mother is struggling with too."

"Of course. That's understandable. But this isn't forever. You both will heal and will move forward. Which way you move forward with the relationship with your mother is up to you."

"You heard what she said. ... She's glad he is gone. Yet they loved each other once. I know they did. And still he seemed to have no problem doing that to us." Opal tried to hold back her tears.

"It's okay if you cry."

"I can, but it doesn't solve anything." Stepping away from him, apparently trying to give herself a bit of distance, she stared again at the cookies.

"Any chance of a pot of coffee to go with a couple of those?"

She shook her head at him and laughed. "I don't think even you can eat all these. What was I thinking?"

"I don't think you *were* thinking. On the other hand, we're quite grateful to be the recipients. Besides, between me and Reyes, we can totally pound down these babies in no time."

She smiled. "I forgot how insanely nice you are."

He groaned. "Are we back to those damaging insults again?"

She looked up at him, tears in her eyes, as she whispered, "No insults, just the truth."

He opened his arms once again, and she walked into them and started to bawl. It started off as tiny sobs, barely shoulder-shaking, until the grief was ripped out of her in great big soul-shattering shakes and ugly bawling.

He held her close, as every sound broke his heart. Every movement of her body, every cry wrenched from so deep in her soul, it was all he could do to hold back his own tears, as he realized how much pain she'd been through and how much was still to come, as the truth would unfold eventually.

But she was strong, stronger than anybody he knew. When she finally slowed down and stood in his arms, he held her close, not letting her go, even when she tried to pull back. Finally, when she made a second attempt, he let her have enough room to lift her head.

She stared up at him. "Whew. I guess I needed that, but I didn't need to do it all over you."

"You needed it, and apparently you *did* need to do it over me, so I'm totally okay with that."

She gave him a lopsided smile. "We're back to that part about you being a really nice man."

He leaned over, kissed her gently on the forehead, and replied, "Besides, I'm somebody who loves you. That's all. Now, can I have some coffee?"

And that made her giggle. "God, I'm such a mess."

"You're a mess, but you're a mess that's healing."

"I don't think so," she murmured. "It feels as if it's all bad, and nothing will ever be good again."

"Yet it will be," Steven stated. "Maybe not today, maybe not tomorrow, but you will eventually start to find peace in your heart again."

She took a deep breath. "The fact that they dumped me overboard and sent me to the bottom of the ocean, throwing me away, as if a piece of garbage, is something that I struggle with."

"And dealing with that will be one of your challenges."

"I can't even imagine having children. The thought of adding anybody to this world that's so messed up and is so sick, knowing that my child could be targeted like that, I just can't." She shook her head.

"It's a good thing that's not an issue right now." He stopped and looked at her in mock horror. "Or is it?"

She stared at him, unblinking for a moment, not comprehending, and then she started laughing. "No, it's not an issue. I am not pregnant."

"Good, because all this coffee and cookies wouldn't be good for your unborn child."

"Thank God I don't have one." She shook her head. "I could definitely plow into a couple of these cookies."

"Yeah, but you'll plow into a couple," he teased, "whereas I will plow into a couple dozen."

As soon as he had the coffee, he proved to her exactly what he meant. And it didn't take any effort at all. He didn't know what baking she did when she wasn't upset, but, man, the cookies were to die for. He carried a plate with just four cookies on it into the living room, and Reyes took one look and reached eagerly for all four, Steven knew that it would be a case of survival-of-the-fittest. Otherwise there wouldn't be enough cookies for the two of them.

When she took a look at the empty plate seconds later, she burst out laughing. "There are more," she murmured.

"I'm glad to hear that," Reyes tattled, "because Steven didn't share very well."

She looked over at Steven in mock outrage.

He protested, "Honestly, he took all four." But since

they were already gone, he knew that there was a good chance she wouldn't believe him. He hopped back up, ran into the kitchen, refilled the plate with a dozen cookies, and brought it back out, putting it down in front of them.

"Now there's enough for both of us." Steven glared at Reyes, who gave him an impudent grin.

"And now here's the coffee," Opal said, coming up behind him. As she sat down, she looked over at Reyes. "Any news?"

He shook his head. "Not yet, but we have a lot of feelers out."

"A lot of feelers, *huh*? That seems to be another way to say, *Nothing is happening.*"

"And yet we got Marshal back," he murmured, looking at her sideways.

"It's stupid," she admitted, "but everything is taking so long, and it reminds me of when he … It doesn't matter."

Reyes stopped eating and studied the cookie in his hand. "You don't want to hear this, and it could very well be why the other two want you to open that box from your father. So, is there any chance that it might shed light on the case?"

Opal stared at him, her throat working, and then she nodded. "I was thinking the same thing, which is also why I didn't want to open it, because, damn, it's like … a time bomb."

"Time bombs are the most dangerous before they're opened," Steven said gently, "but, at least once they're opened and you discharge their contents, they can't hurt you anymore."

"But, as long as they're locked up in their little box, they can't hurt me at all."

He nodded slowly. "I get that. I do, and, if you can live

with not knowing, that's up to you."

Reyes looked at him sharply, then his gaze went over to Opal, waiting …

"No, that's not fair." She pulled it out from her pocket, stared at it, took a deep breath, and finally said, "I need to open it."

"You do," Steven confirmed. He stood by her side, looking at the small black box. Bigger than a ring box, it was taped securely shut. "Yet you also have some time. So, if you don't want to do it right now, then don't."

"But what am I waiting for? I'll open it."

Chapter 10

O PENING THE BOX wasn't quite so easy though. Opal studied it for a long moment and then tried to rip off the tape, but it wouldn't budge.

"I don't know what he put it together with," she murmured, "but it's not easy to open."

"I'll get you a knife." Steven walked into the kitchen, only to return while munching on another cookie, but he was holding a knife in his other hand. She glared at him. "Did you really steal another cookie?"

"Nope, I didn't steal it. You told me to help myself."

She grinned at him. "Remember? There's chocolate cake for dessert."

"Perfect." He grinned. "And, no, I won't ruin my dinner by eating it now."

She shook her head, looked over at Reyes. "Do you eat like he does?"

"I don't usually get a chance because I'm not around the same jobs, but like most of the guys I work with, and from what I remember of Steven"—Reyes chuckled—"he takes it all."

She nodded. "I noticed."

At that, all of a sudden, the seal on the box gave way, and she stared at the lid now in her hand. Whatever was inside the box was hidden from view with tissue paper.

"Is this some jewelry? I'm not sure I have ever received jewelry from my father." She frowned. She took a deep breath and then slowly lifted the tissue paper and stared in absolute and complete shock. On another piece of tissue paper was an absolutely massive pink diamond. She sank back onto the couch. "My God," she whispered, staring in awe at the magnificent jewel.

"That's some kind of inheritance," Reyes whispered, leaning forward with a low whistle.

She stared at it. "Is this what everybody is looking for?" she asked. "Is that why they kidnapped Marshal?"

"I don't know," Steven said. "Is there anything else in the box?"

She looked at him blankly and then slowly lifted the diamond, staring at it. "My God," she muttered. "All I can think about is that this is stolen goods."

"But you don't know that," Steven said quietly. "You can't judge him for that. He worked a lifetime with not much left. For all you know, that was his retirement fund."

She nodded slowly. "No, I don't." Holding the diamond in one hand, she lifted the tissue paper it rested on and found a folded piece of paper under it. She pulled it out and, under the paper, was a small gold key. She held it out to Steven. "I have no idea what that's for."

"No, but *that* is exactly what everybody will be looking for. Not to mention the diamond." He studied the diamond, shook his head, looked over at Reyes. "That's got to be worth millions."

Reyes turned to Opal. "May I?"

After another quick look, she handed it over.

Reyes estimated, "Double-digit millions. We can ask Di. She'll have a good idea." He started taking pictures of it.

"Plus," Opal suggested, "something this size is probably well documented. There would be a provenance, certificates of its history."

Reyes nodded. "We already have somebody we can get answers from." Reyes, with Steven's help, took several photos of the jewel on his phone, using various items to give a size reference, then quickly downloaded his cell phone pictures on his laptop. Within minutes he was typing up an email. After attaching the photos, he hit Send.

Opal watched as Reyes turned to Steven, who had turned the key over several times and now took photos of it.

For Opal, the note ripped her apart, before she even opened it to read it. "It's not big enough to be an explanation," she muttered. "And God knows that's what I really want from him. This"—she waved it around—"can't offer anything I need to hear."

"You don't know that. It could be the first of many such letters. You don't know where this key is from, and it could hold all the answers. You don't know anything yet," Steven warned. "You need to open that note, and you need to see if it explains anything."

She nodded but didn't move. Then finally opened it up and whispered, "There are numbers on it. Numbers. Just numbers." And she gave it to Steven.

He looked at the note and gave a fat grin, with a knowing look at Reyes, who watched him. He passed off the note, turned to Opal, adding, "I know what the number is. Where did your father bank?"

"I don't know." She shrugged. "The lawyer would know. Likely my mom as well."

"Okay, more to the point, where did *you* bank?"

"The one I've always used. As a matter of fact, my father

opened the account with me." She raised an eyebrow at the grin on his face. "Why?"

"Good," he said. He got up and asked Reyes, "Can you hold down the fort here?"

"Yeah, but I really don't like you going without backup though."

"I know, especially after the lawyer has been here," Steven admitted. He frowned, as he thought about it. "Yet I'm not sure I want anybody to know about it either," he said, pointing upstairs. He looked over at her. "Agreed?"

Opal frowned at them both.

"Until we get to the bottom of it, you don't tell them anything." Reyes voiced his concern.

"Fine, but you're worrying about nothing." At least Opal hoped it was nothing. She placed the rock back in the box, then shook her head. "My God. That is gorgeous."

"Do you have a safe deposit box?"

"I do," she said, "but nothing's in it though."

"There's about to be something in it. Come on. Let's go." With that, and pictures of everything from the box sent to Levi, Steven walked out to the car with her, holding the gem in his pocket. The box she left on the coffee table with Reyes, so no one would have a clue what they had. In her pocket, she carried the key and the note.

"Just for the record, I don't think this is a good idea," she said, pulling down the car mirror in front of her. "Look at my face. It's not as if I can hide this. Not to mention I'll attract extra attention and will likely struggle to get anyone to understand that I am who I say I am."

"I know, but I can't do this without you."

Then he drove her down to the bank. She walked in and, because of her facial swelling, her ID was checked, then double-checked, as Steven explained about the car accident she'd been in. Technically cleared, they were led to a small room to wait. When the bank teller returned, she carried Opal's safe deposit box and promptly left them alone. She put the diamond inside for safekeeping. With that done, he called her back and now asked for box number 1472.

The bank teller frowned at Steven, and he shrugged. "We needed to do something with hers first."

The teller nodded, taking away the first box, leaving to retrieve the second safe deposit box. She was back just a moment later with box 1472.

As soon as the teller left once again, Opal's breath gushed out in a *woosh*. "I didn't really believe those numbers would be another safe deposit box," she murmured quietly. Seeing it here in front of her was confirmation of her father's message. She stared at it. "It feels like Pandora's box is facing me right now. I didn't really think he would do this."

"I did. But now this *is* the tricky part."

"Right," she whispered. "What the hell is in here?" She opened it slowly, as if snakes were inside. Right off the bat, there was something she didn't want to see. A handgun. Steven pulled out plastic gloves from his pocket, quickly donning them, and picked up the gun, checked it out. "It's empty, maybe recently fired, but that's hard to say." Then he set it on the table. Underneath were wads of cash. She stared at it.

He lifted them out and looked at them, then called Reyes and said, "I'm sending you a bunch of pictures." And he started taking photographs of everything inside the box. By the time he got all the cash out, he estimated it was fifty thousand plus.

"So much for being broke," she muttered.

"It's nothing compared to what he might have had though," he reminded her.

"Yeah, but that diamond is worth everything, I guess." When the cash was out, at the bottom of the box was a small book. Steven picked it up and looked over at her.

She nodded. "Have at it. See if it means anything to you because I seriously have no clue."

He nodded and took a look at the book, while she went through the rest of the box. There were notes, some other papers, his passport, and a second passport in another name. She winced at that. "You really were planning on leaving us, weren't you, Dad?"

Then, as if in an answer to her question, she found a letter on the bottom with her name on the envelope. Holding it up, she showed it to Steven.

He took a photo of it, before she opened it, and then handed it back to her. "Now take a look."

"Here?" she asked nervously.

"Definitely here. And I'll get a picture of the words too."

Understanding that, once they left, things could be very different, she opened up the letter and laid it down. Steven took several photos of it. It was a single page, but written on both sides, addressed to her. She took a deep breath and read it out loud.

"Dear Opal,

"I don't know how you feel about me at this point. I never wanted to hurt you. I didn't even intend to go down this pathway. Somehow it happened. But, once it had, I couldn't stop it. And it became an easy way to feel empowered in a world that was so messed up, where the criminals I put behind bars didn't stay there and where the ones I helped to get convicted were released after minimum to no time in jail. It seemed as if

everything was so wrong, and yet this money was suddenly there, and it felt so right.

"Once I made that first step, everything else changed for me. I know that you probably can't excuse anything I've done, and, only because of the lawyer do I have a chance to even leave this for you. And I don't even have time to give you much of an explanation.

"The diamond is yours. Do with it what you want; it's fully legal. When I knew that I was losing everything, I cashed in most of the money I had saved that I was planning on leaving to your mother, but instead I leave to you. That is the cash in this safe deposit box.

"It has been painful to watch her and Marshal, knowing they wanted to be together, yet neither one of them was prepared to take the first step to make it happen. I had to do it for them. Marshal has always been head over heels in love with her. Somewhere along the line, I fell out of love, and I don't even know when or how. Maybe it was watching her and Marshal moon over each other. It was pathetic and painful.

"At the same time, it also gave me the impetus to move forward and to change my life. I didn't think it would blow up like it did. I never thought I would end up in jail for this. But of course I did. The good guys end up getting convicted, and the bad guys get off. At least I'd like to think I'm still one of the good guys.

"I worked with a group, other cops and other criminals. These are dangerous men, I don't want you to have anything to do with. I wouldn't even be leaving this for you, but, once I'm dead and gone, I'm hoping they won't care. Do I know that I'll die? No, but I'm assuming I won't live more than a few weeks, a few months—maybe, if I'm lucky, surely not more than a year in prison. My time is up. It's over.

"Would I have changed it? Hell, yes, I would have. If I had

it to do over, I would have divorced your mother a long time ago, and I would have found another way to make peace with the work I did, or I would have left the job entirely. I did find somebody else for a time, but that didn't work out either. I knew I had to leave and had to do something that would make me feel better about my life. If you are wondering if this was the answer, no, it wasn't, but it's the one that I found, and it's the one that I stuck with, and it's the one I'm paying the ultimate price for.

"*However, you don't have to. This is your money; this is for you. It's legal too. I can't make it any better. The notebook gives you all the cops I worked with, who are just as bad as I am. It gives you the names of everybody I worked with on the criminal side as well. You'll have to hand this over to somebody pretty high up in law enforcement because, as you'll see from the names, an awful lot of people have good reasons for me not to live.*"

Opal murmured in distress, losing the nerve to continue.

Steven motioned for her to continue and smiled encouragingly.

"*I'm not naming names, while I go to jail. There's no point. They won't believe me, and those above me will make sure that I don't survive to tell the tale, so I left a record. A record that is as upright and as honest as you are. You will make sure it gets into the right hands. I am so sorry to leave you with this burden. It's not what I wanted at any time.*

"*Know this. You are not responsible for my mistakes, and your mother is not responsible either. I sincerely hope that she and Marshal will have a good life together. Marshal was never involved in any of this. This was me, just me, and, of course, every name in that book. Know that I love you, and I always did. Spend the money wisely.*

"*Love, your father*"

Steven heard the words, and it made him feel a hell of a

lot better to know that Marshal wasn't involved. It still didn't completely clear him of everything that happened afterward, but it was good to know. As Steven watched her, big fat tears rolled down her cheeks. She looked up at him, wordless, and once again he opened his arms and held her close.

"My God," she whispered, "why couldn't he have told me any of this in jail?"

"Because he was being watched," Steven said quietly against her ear, "and all the phone calls and visits are recorded."

"Oh my God." Opal trembled in his arms. "This is so painful."

"It is painful, but it's also freeing." He tilted her head back and smiled down at her. "You have answers, and you have knowledge that he knew and understood what he did, maybe not why he did it, but understanding that, once he headed down this path, there was no getting away from it. And he took whatever precautions he could for you."

"So, do I get to keep this?"

He nodded. "We'll have to take a closer look at everything that's happened, but he said that he cashed out everything of his, and I presume he had a 401k and the other types of regular pensions."

She nodded. "Yes, but surely that won't have anything to do with this, would it?"

"It's hard to say. But he knew that dirty money would only be a burden to you, and he said as much. Did he ever inherit anything?"

She shook her head. "Maybe his father's estate, but I don't know how much it was worth."

"I suspect we'll find out that it was enough for this, although that diamond is worth millions."

"And maybe that was part of the estate too," she added. "My grandfather was a jeweler."

"Then that is quite possible," Steven said. "It will be secure here in the safe deposit box, and we have taken photos of all this, which we're sending to Levi for safekeeping."

"That's why they're after me, right?"

"It is. And you know what it is they're after, right?"

She stared at him uncomprehendingly, and he lifted the book.

She winced. "Right, so he had this book and was holding it over them."

"I don't even know if he was holding it over them," Steven clarified, "but to know there *was* a book also meant that everybody had to look for it, or else."

"So, even in the end, he did the right thing," she whispered. She watched and ended up helping Steven slowly and methodically take pictures of each and every page of the book, sending them to Reyes and Levi both. "There, that takes some of the pressure off."

He smiled at her. "Yes, I would say so. Now we have to get that information to somebody who can do something about it. I don't know all the names in here, but I presume that having gone to as much trouble as he has, there's an awful lot of people very high up who will be very unhappy that the book has been found. Hence contacting Levi at the same time. If he doesn't know who to contact already, he'll find the right person."

She nodded. "I hope every last one of them goes to prison," she said viciously. "Particularly the one who dumped me overboard and sent me to the bottom of the ocean, as if I had no value at all."

He nodded. "Again, we'll have to make sure that you are safe, while this all comes out in the open. Once people realize that the book has been found, they won't be looking at you anymore."

When his phone rang, he checked his cell, but the reception was really terrible in the vault area. He looked at her, "Do you want any of this right now?"

She shook her head. "No, why don't we leave it all until ... except for the letter. I want the letter."

Since he'd already gotten a photo of it, he nodded. "I'll leave the book here, as I've already taken images of every page. We will leave all the evidence here, where it's safe."

"Good." She stepped back and stared at her father's safe deposit box. "My God. I still can't believe it."

"You see? In a way this turned out to be the best-case scenario."

She frowned at him and then nodded slowly. "It really is."

"That voice from the past is really hard to accept, but, once you realize where he was at and what he did and why, and what he's done at the end of the day, in a way it's a gift."

"It's a huge gift," she murmured. "I still don't feel safe now."

"And that's why everything is staying here. Everything has been photographed and has gone to Levi. My texts aren't going through. We have to step out of here so that can happen."

"We have to save the key," she murmured. At that, they rang for the teller to come back, and she asked for her box again. And, with that box, she quickly placed the key and the code inside. Steven had already taken a photo of that as well. "Now, the most important part," she said, "is keeping your phone safe."

He grinned at her. "As soon as we have clearance from here, everything will fly off into the internet, and believe me. Once it's there, there is no going back. Phone or no phone."

The two of them, arms around each other—and with her still sniffling a bit, but with a much lighter heart—stepped out of the vault.

HE LED HER outside the bank, knowing that getting home and getting her safely away from here was now paramount. But they had the information, and very quickly it would all blow up. But he also had no doubt that somebody could easily have followed them here. Even the knowledge of what they now knew was dangerous. He hustled her into the vehicle.

"What's the rush now?" she asked, as she reached for the seat belt.

"Instinct."

She immediately slid lower in the front seat of the car. "Do you think we were followed?"

"I wouldn't be at all surprised," he said, looking in the rearview mirror. "What I don't know is who would have followed us."

"Right," she muttered. "The house is probably being watched, isn't it?"

"There's been too many things going on around us to not consider that," he murmured. She fell silent at his side. He looked over at her and smiled, as he pulled out of the parking lot. "Let's get you home."

"And what if they do find us? Or follow us home? I can't lead them there. They'll want answers and won't care how they get them."

"But now we can tell them that everything is in the hands of the cops."

"Is it?"

He checked his phone. "Levi has copies of all of it now." Even as he spoke, Levi called. Steven put the phone on Speaker. "Hey, Levi. I'm here with Opal. We've just left the bank, heading home now."

"Really nice job on finding all that," Levi said, his voice strong, determined. "It'll take us a bit to figure out who to contact. Some pretty big names are on here."

"I figured as much. It's also why I think Roscoe set this up so that he didn't go down alone."

"Of course not," Levi muttered. "However, now that we have the information, it's really important that you keep her safe, until we can get it out into the public domain, plus getting everybody picked up."

"I know," Steven said, looking around the area. "I want to get her back to the house."

"Even that's not necessarily a good location," Levi murmured.

"I need to go home for my mother's sake," Opal said, leaning forward to speak into the phone.

Levi paused for a moment. "I hear you. Any chance I can convince you to get out of there very quickly?"

"Do you think the house will be targeted?" she asked worriedly, looking at Steven in alarm.

"Honestly, I'm afraid you won't even make it there," Levi said bluntly. "If anybody knows you were at a safe deposit box, that'll set off all kinds of alarms."

"Of course it could, yet everything looks safe at the moment." She frowned, twisting to look behind them.

Everything looked normal. "Steven, don't you agree?"

"No," he said to the phone, "all my senses are on full alert."

"But I don't see anything," she cried out softly, twisting and turning frantically.

"You're not supposed to see them when they come," he said quietly. "I don't know who or what it is. We're trying to avoid trouble, so it could come from anywhere."

She gasped at that. "We're only a few minutes from home."

"Right," Levi replied. "Let me know if you end up in any trouble at home. Otherwise pack and call me. I've already given Reyes the heads-up to move Ruby and Marshal. Meanwhile, we'll make arrangements for you to disappear for a while."

Steven added, "We need a place, somewhere in town, where nobody would know."

"We can arrange that," Levi answered, "and I'd just as soon you went there right now instead of home."

As they drove toward home, Steven suddenly changed lanes and made a quick left turn. "I'm making an executive decision here. Levi, find us a place fairly close and register us under a different name. We are not going home."

"What?" she asked, staring at him, hanging onto the door, as he took another sharp turn.

"No time to argue," he snapped, turning the wheel hard again. "Everything inside me is screaming for me to get you the hell away from here."

"Good decision." Levi's voice, calm and steady, rolled through the car. "Stay on the line. Ice is getting you a location."

"I think we're being followed," Steven immediately said,

cutting through the conversation. Then he looked at the rearview mirror and swore.

Opal twisted to look behind them.

"What vehicle?" Levi asked.

"A black truck. We're driving her mother's car."

"Of course," Levi noted. "That would be another one they would track."

"The rental SUV is at the house. I left it there to avoid anybody seeing us picking it up. So we had a vehicle they didn't know about."

"Once they lost track of Reyes, it probably didn't make a damn bit of difference."

"It was on my list to switch vehicles, but I hadn't done it yet."

"Yeah, Steven's been a little busy," she said to Levi, and even he could recognize the panic in her voice.

"They're behind us, but that doesn't mean they have us," Steven said.

"No, but they're closing in." She twisted to look back.

"Opal, look at me. I need you to stay calm, and I need you to stay quiet," Steven said, "I've got to drive, and Levi is trying to find us a place to go."

"But no point in getting us a new place if they'll follow us there," she said, her voice shaky but at least muted.

"Oh, please, have a little faith." Steven chuckled.

Even Levi had a smile in his voice when he said, "Remember, Opal. Everybody on my team is trained for this kind of thing."

"I get that. I really do, but damn …" And, with that, she settled back, staring at the rearview mirror. "He's getting closer."

"Yep."

"Why? Will he hit us?" she asked.

"He'll try." Steven made a quick right-hand turn around the block and quickly evaded him. The truck was traveling too fast and overshot the corner.

"Oh, he's gone." Opal cheered and laughed.

"No, he's not gone," Steven corrected. He shifted around, coming back onto the same road again. "We've done a series of rights, so we're back on the same road. He'll be here at our side very quickly."

"Are you sure?" she asked.

"Yeah, I am sure, and that's another reason why I'm not taking you home. Levi, can you check on Reyes? Get them out of there."

"Yeah, we've already got that in progress. So far, he hasn't picked up."

"He's there with my mom." Opal started to panic. "We have to go home."

"No," Steven said, trying to keep his voice reasonable, as he quickly took another series of turns. "We are not going home."

"I can't let her get hurt. What if they throw her overboard too?"

"Remember. You have to trust me."

She took several slow deep breaths, but her fingers were clenched so tightly that her nails would start cutting through the skin. But that was all he could give her, as he was busy evading the tailing vehicle, as it came up and around behind them again.

Steven quickly switched lanes and hit his brakes, even as horns honked around them, but the truck once again overshot them, and Steven was now behind him. "Now I'm on his tail," he told Levi, and Steven quickly read off the license plate to Levi. "I could use a hand to corner this asshole. Anyone close by?"

"Not close." There was a moment of silence coming from Levi's end of the call. "The truck was stolen early this morning. We've just contacted the cops and told them where you are. Should be some distraction soon." Levi added, "We're still trying to figure out who we should be talking to here."

"Check the book for one of the big names that you know, someone you can get some help with." Steven gave a hard laugh. "As long as his name is not there, you should be good to go."

"We do have a lot of people who we know we can trust, but I'm definitely making an extra point of checking the book to confirm that." A few long stretched-out seconds later, Levi said, "Okay, we have somebody we can call. Ice is on it."

"Good." Steven spun the vehicle hard to the left. "These guys are not giving up."

"Can you see the driver?" Levi asked.

"No, I can't," Steven murmured. He looked over at Opal, who was completely frozen in panic. "Opal can't see anything either."

"That's not true," she said in a faint whisper. "I'm here. I'm trying to look." And she was trying, and, for that, he would give her credit. He knew the memories of what these animals had done to her would push her to do what she needed to do.

"He's tall, white, wearing a plaid shirt. Maybe with ... red hair and a beard."

"Good," Levi said. "I can use that. Remember. The cops are looking for that stolen vehicle. Not that it would give you instant relief, but it would at least help us track him." And, with that, the phone went quiet for a moment.

"Did he leave?" Opal cried out. "Where's Levi?"

Levi came on the line again. "I'm right here. Steven, Ice has you located, and we have satellite surveillance on you now."

"That won't necessarily help," Steven said, but he had already taken an exit off the freeway. "We are now heading into the north side of Fort Bragg. A pub's over here for a landmark. Otherwise I can keep driving and head out on the freeway for a few hours."

"That's up to you," Levi said. "You tell me what you need to do."

"I'll let you know in a bit," he said, as he saw the vehicle coming up behind them. "Assholes," he muttered.

"There they are again. They're staying on your tail, and that's good." Levi chuckled. "You might want to drive them right to the police station."

At that, Steven laughed. "Not a bad idea." He made a series of turns again and completely lost them. And, when he was ready to relax ever-so-slightly, he saw them come up behind him again, some two cars behind him. He told Levi, "Okay, if you've got the local police station prepped, I'm about two miles away."

"Yeah, got you a couple miles away from the PD per satellite feed," Levi confirmed. "Take your pursuer in on the far side if you can, drive them right up into the big lot in the back. Believe me. A lot of people are waiting for them."

And that's what Steven did, although it wasn't that easy or that fast. However, by the time he had his tail so confused about where he was, Steven made several more turns and raced into the rear of a parking lot, coming in the back way.

As soon as he did that, the other vehicle came right up behind him on his tail. Almost immediately Steven hit the brakes.

Gunfire from the truck peppered the car, but Steven had Opal flat on the floorboard, with return fire coming fast and heavy outside. Steven waited for a long moment. "Well, Levi," he said quietly, "we're fine, but I'm not sure about anybody else."

"Stand down," Levi said.

Suddenly shouts from outside called Steven to step out of the vehicle, with his hands up.

"Are those your guys?" Steven asked Levi, watching as dozens of cops showed up.

"They're cops," Levi said, with a note of humor. "It's standard procedure whenever there's open fire."

"Yeah, too bad I didn't get a chance to return fire." Steven looked around and said, "I want to make sure they're not bad cops."

"Yeah," Levi added. "Somebody else is racing outside right now on your behalf, so remain in the vehicle."

Finally somebody came up to the vehicle, tapped the window, stepped back, and ordered them out.

Steven helped Opal out of the vehicle on his side, noting at least a half-dozen cops standing around.

"That's good news," he murmured to her quietly.

She frowned at him. "What's good about this?" She quivered in his arms. He held her tight. "Any one of them can be bad."

"Absolutely, but the chances of them *all* being crooked is slim, and, if there is even one, he won't do anything when everybody else is here watching."

"Oh." She relaxed ever-so-slightly.

His gaze wandered, closely looking at all the men in front of them. He didn't know how many were involved in this, if any, and that was something that had to be kept in mind too. Just because they were cops didn't mean they were bad, and Steven had no idea how many policemen were listed in Roscoe's book, but Steven thought it was about fifty from different departments. Quite a few men from this department were in front of them right now.

"It's all good," he said, holding her close. They were slowly led inside the police station. When they were taken to a specific room, he nodded and pulled two chairs up close and sat down.

"Are we in trouble?" she asked, sitting right beside him, half wrapped in his arms.

"If there was any trouble, chances are, we would have been separated."

She shuddered at that. "I don't think I could have stood that," she whispered.

When the door opened suddenly a few minutes later, Steven looked over at the man and said, "Please identify yourself."

He nodded and pulled out his badge and held it out for Steven to see. "Now," the detective said, lifting his phone, "this is probably who you want to hear from." He lifted his phone to his lips and stated, "Levi, I'm in the room with them." He then handed his phone to Steven.

At that, Steven grabbed it. "Levi?"

"Yeah, I'm here." Levi delivered the news Steven waited to hear. "That was Detective Richardson. He's one of our contacts, and he's on your side."

"That's good to know," Steven stated. "An awful lot of people were out there."

"There were," Levi confirmed. "Believe me. The chaos is just starting. We are rounding up the names on the list. I'm not sure all of them are on duty, and nobody is talking, not until they get everybody picked up."

"That makes sense," Steven murmured. He handed the phone back to the detective. "Nice to meet you."

"Always a pleasure to work with Levi, but it would be damn nice if we didn't have him in our territory all the time." He said goodbye and hung up the call.

"If shit didn't keep happening, you wouldn't have to," Steven replied in a hard tone of his own.

Richardson nodded. Then he looked over at Opal and sighed. "This again, *huh?*"

She nodded slowly. "Yeah, this again," she said bitterly. "I'm not sure how many of your cohorts out there were involved, but somebody tried to murder me. They threw me overboard into the ocean with cement blocks on my feet and a rope tied around my neck. So, believe me. I'll see this to the end to ensure I can have a life after this."

He studied her battered face for a long moment and nodded. "Levi told me, and I couldn't believe anybody would do that. There's also no copy of your file."

"As I've found out the hard way, not all the cops are good guys." And such bitterness filled her tone that the detective winced.

"We're not all bad though." He smiled gently. "I get it. You've been to hell and back with your own father and with whoever did this to you"—he waved his hands in the air—"but we aren't all the same."

She sagged back and whispered, "I know. I'm sorry. I'm not trying to be a terrible person. I'm exhausted and worried, and I want to make sure my family is okay."

At that, he looked over at Steven. "Is there a problem with her family?"

"We aren't sure," Steven said. "My partner is at the safe house alone with her mother and Marshal, her father's partner."

"Ah, Marshal," Detective Richardson repeated, but a thoughtful tone filled his voice. "Is he on your suspect list?"

"Of course, but not in Roscoe's black book," Steven explained. "Until we get to the end of this and have it all sorted out, Marshal remains on my suspect list."

Richardson nodded. "Understood."

"I know why you are still suspicious," Opal admitted to Steven, "but my father did say that Marshal wasn't involved."

"He did?" Richardson turned to her.

"Yeah, he left me a letter in the safe deposit box," she said, with a quiet explanation.

"Now *that* I would like to see."

She nodded. "And, when this is over, and you have imprisoned all those assholes named in that book of his, then you can see it." He looked at her, not liking what she had to say. She shook her head. "No," she stated. "I've been to hell and back over this, and, if it wasn't for Marshal, I would be another statistic of a missing person and fish food for the bottom of the marina," she murmured. "I'm not going through that again."

"Got it."

Then the door opened again, and somebody with a whole lot more brass and authority stepped in. He looked over at Steven. "You guys really like bringing shit to my town, don't you?"

"Not really. The shit was already here." Steven stood,

giving the man a straightforward look. "But if there wasn't shit that had to be dealt with from bad cops, it wouldn't be such a problem."

He nodded slowly. "Yes, I'm here at Levi's request." He glared at Steven. "What kind of a shitstorm has he found this time?" Then he looked over at Opal, and his eyebrows shot up, when he saw her swollen and bruised face. "What happened to you?" he probed.

"Yeah," she snorted, "courtesy of somebody involved in this mess." Opal then carefully recounted what happened to her.

His face paled when he realized that she'd being thrown overboard and that Marshal had brought her back. "Good God," he cried out. "What the hell is this all about?"

"A little black book with all the names," Steven added in a low tone.

At that, the boss man nodded. "Right, and we're working on that, but I'll need a copy of that book."

"You only get photocopies of the pages." Steven shook his head. "Until I know that Opal's safe and sound, that book does not leave where it's currently hidden."

He stared at him in anger, clearly offended.

"Levi gave you copies of everything already. If that's not enough for you now, then you don't understand how she's feeling about what was done to her."

When he took another look at her black and blue face, he winced. "Right."

"We also have a security problem with her mother and Marshal. I haven't heard from my partner, who was with them at her safe house."

"A cruiser has been sent over. I haven't received an update yet, but we are investigating that right now."

"I would feel better if I was there," Steven said. At that, Opal cried out and grabbed his hand, clutching it tightly. He shook his head and added, "I'm not leaving you."

"Can we go together?" She turned and glared at the two men. "You can't keep us here, can you?"

The head guy shook his head. "No. You're not under arrest, but obviously we have a lot of questions," he said, with emphasis. "But considering that somebody's still out there possibly causing trouble, and we're still trying to pick up all the names in that little book, if you need to go, ... then go." He stepped out of the way. "However, we'll expect to see you back here tomorrow."

Steven nodded. "That's fair."

He knew that they didn't want to let him go, but it's not as if they had a reason to hold him. He grabbed her hand and helped her to her feet. "Come on. Let's go find your mother." And, with that, they bolted from the room.

When she got out to the car again, she asked him, "Is something wrong?"

"I'm not sure"—Steven swore under his breath—"but it feels very much as if something's not right."

She stared at him during the whole drive. As they got out at the safe house, she saw a cruiser was already there. "Oh, thank God, the cops are here." As she walked into the front door, she saw Reyes, but he didn't look very well. "Are you okay?"

He stared at her grimly. "Did you guys get everything?"

She nodded. "Yes, and Levi has copies of everything, and now so does the brass down at the station. They're picking up everybody as we speak."

"Right. Did you recognize any names in there?"

She shook her head. "Other than a few first names that

were John, which I took note of, I don't think so, why?"

"Any chance that your mom might have known about that diamond?"

"I don't really know. Why?"

"Because she is the one who gave me this." Reyes pointed to the lump on his head.

Chapter 11

O PAL STARED AT him in shock. "Oh, no, no, no, no," she cried out, her hand to her mouth, as she stared at Reyes in horror. "Please, no."

He nodded. "I'm sorry, but, yes, she did. She also specifically mentioned the diamond, as she slammed something onto my head. Something about how it's hers. She deserves it, for all she went through."

"I didn't even know anything about it before now, so how could she?" Opal asked. "I don't understand why she would do that."

"I think to make good on her escape plan." Reyes looked over at Steven.

"Does that mean she's involved in all this?" Opal asked in a tiny voice. Steven stepped up, his arm going around her shoulders. She looked up at him, tears welling in her eyes. "She brought you guys in here in the first place."

He held her close, as he turned a questioning gaze to Reyes.

"I can't answer that," Reyes grumbled. "All I can tell you is that she knocked me out, when I was sitting here working. The last thing I remember was closing my laptop and hearing someone coming up behind me. I turned enough to see her and, *boom*, down I went."

"What about Marshal?" Steven searched the room.

"I don't know." Reyes shrugged. "I honestly don't know, and I'd really like to."

"Surely she wouldn't have been involved in my kidnapping. She wouldn't have done this to me," Opal whispered. She turned to stare at Steven, her last hope dwindling. "Please, God, tell me that she didn't do this."

Reyes sighed. "It's quite possible that she wanted the money or the diamond, so she could cash in and leave. Remember how she felt about being here."

"What's that got to do with me? If she would have mentioned it, I would have given it to her."

"How would she have known about it?" Steven asked, frowning, "Would your father have told your mother about either one?"

"She saw the box," Reyes pointed out. "Then her face went pale, and she got really, really angry."

"Maybe it's something else entirely," Opal weakly argued.

"I don't think she had anything to do with your kidnapping," Steven shared, "but I think that she's on a rampage right now. I honestly don't know if it's connected or not."

Opal hated to even think about it.

"Any idea where they'd have gone?" Steven's gaze encompassed Reyes and Opal. Steven held the keys to Ruby's car in his hand, already walking to the front door. Had they taken Marshal's truck or the rented SUV? Steven glanced outside, looking around, stepped back inside, and shot a hard gaze at Reyes. "Keep her here." And, with that, he disappeared, slamming the door behind him.

She raced to open it, only to hear Reyes's commanding order. "Stop."

Pivoting, she stared at him. "He's going after them. I

should be with him."

"No," he ordered in a steely voice. "This needs to be completely separate from you. This is now a criminal matter. Part of the ongoing investigation. Unfortunately your mother's actions have put you right back into the danger zone and you again in the cops' spotlight. You need to understand. The cops arrived to make sure your family was safe, only to find me out cold on the floor. There isn't any way to sweep this under the carpet. Not now."

Her hands went to her mouth, as tears formed in the corners of her eyes. "I'm sorry. I wasn't thinking of you. She did assault you. And while you're already injured from before."

He waved that off. "The police will decide that. And, speaking of which, they want to talk to you. So while Steven goes and hunts down Ruby and Marshal, you will stay here with me and talk to the cops."

She sagged into an armchair.

The back door opened, and several officers stepped in. They nodded at her, their gazes hard as they studied her puffy face.

"Glad to see you," the first one said. "We need to ask you a few questions."

"What about?" she asked, glancing to Reyes, then back again.

"Everything. Your father. Your attack. The attack on Reyes here."

She closed her eyes, hating what her mother had done, putting Opal back into this position. Finally, searching for and finding that long-lost thread of steel she used to have in her spine, she opened her eyes and nodded. "Go ahead. Ask away."

STEVEN PULLED INTO Marshal's driveway and parked. He saw no vehicle on this side of the house, but the door stood partially open. He jumped up the stairs two at a time and slid inside. He heard voices ahead. From where he stood, he recognized Marshal and Ruby as the speakers. So they hadn't gone far. Steven had figured that, if they were planning to book it, Marshal would still need to pack something. Ruby might be okay to leave with nothing but her purse, but that didn't mean they didn't need a few necessities, like a passport, depending on where they were hoping to go.

Steven had already updated Levi on the way over here, and he was now pissed too.

This was the second attack on Reyes and not one they could ignore this time. So, as soon as Steven dealt with these two, he had to get Reyes checked out at a clinic. Meanwhile Levi was looking for a doctor they could get in to see right now and was bringing the cops here to Marshal's place. And, in some ways, Steven was surprised they weren't here already.

In the distance he thought he heard sirens. Were they coming here?

Sliding along the hallway heading to the kitchen, he stopped when he saw the couple. Marshal was sitting on the outside deck stairs, his head in his hands.

Ruby berated him from behind.

"I didn't mean to hit him," she cried out. "You know that."

"But you did though," he growled. "And we ran. For what? You didn't even snatch the diamond."

"I grabbed the box. I didn't have time to check if it was in it or not." She slumped on the stairs beside him. "Reyes has a hard head."

Marshal glared at her. "You attacked an already injured man."

"I know." Her voice dropped to a whisper. "I hope I didn't hurt him."

He stared at her in shock and frustration. "Of course you hurt him. The question is how badly." He shook his head. "We need to go back and face the music."

"No," she cried out. "They'll arrest me."

Steven shook his head. Of course they should arrest her. That didn't mean they'd charge her. That would depend on Reyes and Levi. And the rest of the case. Extenuating circumstances could easily be overlooked. It's hard to say in this case. Yet, as far as Steven was concerned, that attack deserved punishment.

"We have to," Marshal stated, his voice firm. "We ran, and we shouldn't have. It was wrong."

"Damn it. I need that diamond. I have nothing without it. You know that. The house has to be sold to pay more debts. I won't have anything left."

"But I do," Marshal replied firmly. "And that has to be enough." He stared off in the distance. "He never mentioned the diamond to me at all."

"My father-in-law told me about it," she said. "I never saw it. He said he'd kept a nest egg in case the world collapsed around Roscoe. I've thought of it from time to time, but only when I saw the box did it came crashing back. It's worth millions."

"But it's not yours, and it's not your millions." Marshal reached over and picked up her hand. "We'll get along fine without it. You know that. You're angry and want something to make up for all you've been through. But Opal's pain has been so much worse. And he was her father. It was his family's diamond to pass on. Of course he didn't leave it to you. Not when he knew about us. If I were in his shoes, I would have done the same thing."

"She's young. She doesn't need it. She can work and save. I can't."

He chuckled. "Let's be honest. You could. You don't want to. You're angry, and you have a right to be, but taking it out on Reyes, who was here to help your own daughter at your request? Well, that's not the answer." He stood and hopped down the last couple steps and held out his hand. "Come on."

Just then his gaze lifted, and he caught sight of Steven. His gaze widened and his outstretched arm slowly dropped. "Or not," he whispered, dropping his gaze to Ruby and nodding behind her.

Steven, his arms crossed over his chest, glared at the woman, who jumped to her feet, pivoting to see what was behind her.

She gasped, and the color faded from her face. "I didn't mean it," she cried out, her hand covering her mouth, her eyes bright with tears. "I didn't think. I just reacted." The first tear dropped to slide down her cheek.

Behind him, Steven heard the sirens getting closer.

So could Marshal. He groaned and wrapped his arms around her shoulders. "The cops are coming."

She trembled, but her gaze was locked on Steven. "I'm sorry. So damn sorry."

He nodded. "I bet you are. Now you have to face the consequences. But I don't for one minute think you're sorry for attacking a man from behind, an injured man to boot. Or that the whole point was to steal from your daughter."

Marshal had the good graces to wince, but Ruby stiffened and glared at him.

"Exactly," he said. He motioned behind him. "Shall we?"

Marshal nudged her forward, but she pushed back. "Go where?"

"First, back to the safe house," Steven snapped. "If you refuse, which is your full right, then the policemen who just arrived—after hunting down you both—can arrest you, and you can speak to your daughter down at the station."

She paled. "The police? Are they going to charge me?"

"You think you can attack someone and not face the consequences? Did you really think those cops weren't waiting for you to mess up, so they can dive back into this whole mess again?"

She started shaking.

"That wasn't necessary," Marshal protested.

"But you know it's true." Steven stood with his hands on his hips, waiting for the officers to join him. When they did, he quickly explained, adding, "I want to take them to Reyes and Opal first. Ruby needs to apologize to both of them. Then you can take them both to the station." He turned to face Marshal. "You know how this works and what the charges could mean. And how your behavior at this point on makes a difference. She's coming with me. You can drive your truck back to the house."

"I'm going with Marshal. You can't stop me." Ruby glared at him. "I'm not going with you."

"Fine." He motioned to the officer beside him. "The police can take you there then. Marshal, you will, of course, have an escort."

"Not an issue," he replied. "I have no intention of running."

"Again?" Steven noted, making a point. Steven believed Marshal wouldn't run now, if for no other reason than he wouldn't have Ruby with him. When Ruby screamed, Steven spun around to see Ruby fighting the two officers, moving her to the cruiser. Marshal couldn't get a word in edgewise over her squawks.

Steven had no such qualms. He shoved his face in hers and bellowed, "Stop it."

Silence came, except for the occasional sobs. "I gave you the choice of a dignified return to the safe house, and you spurned it. You no longer can be trusted, along with Marshal, as you both ran after the attack. That leaves traveling in the cruiser. And that's now your *only* option. We can pick you up and carry you if you don't behave."

She shook her head and took several steps forward. "How could you do this? Opal loves you."

"And I love Opal. Too bad you don't. She's been through a massive betrayal from one parent, and now she has to deal with a second parent's betrayal, from the mother who professed to love her."

With that, he turned his back on her, calling out to the cops, "Take her to the safe house. If she causes another scene, take her straight to the station. Book her for resisting arrest as well as assault on my partner and whatever else she has done."

Chapter 12

O PAL FELT AS if she'd never seen her mother before. Or maybe she hadn't seen the real her before. Watching her arrive in a police car, escorted by two officers, who were even now watching her warily, was heartbreaking. The cops delivered her mother to the kitchen, where Opal sat down at the kitchen table and stared at her. "You don't have any right to that diamond. It was part of Daddy's family inheritance."

"Sounds to me like you don't have any right to it," Ruby snapped. "I don't care what he told you. That should have been mine."

"If he'd wanted you to have it, he would have given it to you," Opal said calmly. Yet she wasn't calm inside. She rubbed her temples. "God, what a nightmare."

Marshal stood to the side, staying close to Ruby, but still somewhat distant. "Did you figure anything out?"

"We figured out lots." Steven stepped between Opal and her mother.

Who'd have thought it was necessary, standing between them? Opal thought, as she wondered if his position was on purpose, then realized that, of course, it was. Steven was always that guardian angel. She slid her fingers through his, and his immediately closed around hers. With his other hand, almost in a casual movement that she wanted to feel was deliberate, he snagged another cookie and took a big bite, as he studied the other two in the room.

Opal realized it was almost dinnertime. And, of course, a guy like Steven needed food. "I think your idea earlier is a good one," she whispered. He looked at her, and then she saw the comprehension in his gaze, and he nodded.

"Go upstairs and grab yourself a bag."

She nodded, then, letting go of his hand, she quickly went around behind him and out of the kitchen, leaving her mother spluttering behind her. Trying to block out recent events, Opal entered her bedroom and shut the door.

She packed an overnight bag, not having much to pack, since the move to this rental house had also been quick. In fact, she ended up packing all her belongings. She didn't know where to go with her mother right now, but surely space could only help their relationship. When Opal was ready to leave, she went to the bathroom, grabbed a few toiletries, looked at her face, and cried a few tears. Then stopped.

"Gosh, I am a mess." But it was a mess that she could move on from now. She returned to the bedroom, grabbed her bag, and headed to the door. Her mother blocked the doorway. Opal heard heavy footsteps racing up the stairs. *Steven.*

"Where are you going?" Ruby snapped.

"To a hotel for the night," Opal said. "I want to get away." Her mother crossed her arms over her chest aggressively, but Opal faced her, speaking up to her. "Are you really telling me that you'll stop me? Steven is here, and Reyes. Are you going to attack both of them this time? Me? What about the cops standing outside right now? Even now I don't know if you ever cared about me or Dad or even Marshal. Was it all just about the diamond?" Opal asked.

"Here I thought my life was worth more than that."

"I didn't have anything to do with what they did to you," her mother cried out. "But you know what a nightmare this has been and what that diamond can do for me."

"Sell the house," she snapped. "That will give you plenty of money to start over again. The bills won't take all of it, so you'll have something left over. Start fresh with Marshal."

"But we have to buy another house." She glared at Opal. "It's not as if that'll help."

"Choose someplace where the real estate is cheaper," she muttered, as she tried to brush past her mother.

Ruby grabbed her, her hands almost like claws on Opal's shoulders.

Opal cried out in pain, jerking back, stumbling into the hallway, where strong arms wrapped around her, cradling her closer.

"Look. I'm sorry," Ruby cried out, stepping back from the avenging angel glowering at her. "It was a shock to find out that he gave it to you. I've wondered about that damn thing for years and to hear that he gave it to you …"

"No, I think it wasn't a shock at all. You always knew it was for me. You were hoping that you could get it before I found out," Opal stated, looking her mother directly in the eye. "I want to believe you didn't have anything to do with all this and especially that you had nothing to do with my kidnapping, but right now I'm very confused over it all. I'll work it out over time. However, after what I saw in you today, and what you did to Reyes, I'm not staying here. And, if you want to try and stop me, you can *try*, but I don't think it will be very successful."

A flash of hurt filled her mother's gaze, and she slowly dropped her head. "I didn't mean to hurt Reyes," she said abruptly.

"Maybe you didn't mean to, but you did attack an already injured man," Opal replied. "You knocked him unconscious, and you did it deliberately with the intent to hurt him, and that to me is unbelievable. He was here to protect you. He came at your request to help us—and you attacked him."

"I was angry," she snapped, clenching her fists, then looking down at them and opening them. "I've never been so angry in my life, but, when I saw that jewelry box, and it was open, I knew what must have been in it."

"It doesn't matter if you knew or not," Opal argued, as she headed to the top of the stairs, Steven following close behind. Together they slowly walked downstairs, feeling her whole body ache. Marshal stood near the foot of the stairs, not sure how to proceed. And behind him were the two officers who brought her here.

Opal addressed Marshal. "I'll always be grateful that you saved me," she began, "but right now I'm really confused as to the role you and my mother played in all this. So, for the moment, I'll reserve judgment, and I'll get away for a few days. After what my mother did to Reyes, no way will I stay here. Honestly, I'm not sure I'd sleep a wink, knowing that she had that much anger and hatred in her heart. For all I know, she would tie me up and beat me, just like those men did," she admitted bitterly. "She might hold me captive, until I told her where that stupid diamond was."

Marshal had the grace to look ashamed. "I don't think she would hurt you," he said gently.

"I would have agreed with you yesterday but not today," she noted, as she walked to where Reyes sat.

"Come on." She held out a hand. "I'm not leaving you

here with my mother."

He asked, "Are you sure? She has to go to the station now. They only allowed her to come here, so you could talk to her. That was Steven's doing. We can stay here. She might return tonight, but she might not."

"I don't care where she ends up tonight." Opal did, of course, but right now it was something she couldn't waste her time or energy on. She was too sore and too hurt, both physically and emotionally, to deal with anymore. "Come on. We'll get two rooms." Then she helped him to his feet, and she winced as she saw the size of the lump on his head. "God damn it, that thing is huge. Are you sure we shouldn't get you to the hospital? What did she use on you anyway?" she muttered.

"I don't know for sure." Then Reyes smiled. "At least I got taken out by a woman, so I wouldn't have hit back. If it had been a guy, I'd have felt bad, although being taken out twice out of the blue is a little hard on my ego."

"My mother took advantage of the fact that you were here and that you were comfortable in her home and that you were already injured. All of that is just shitty." And, with that, Opal looked around, frowning, "God, I don't even know how we'll get anywhere. We have no vehicle."

"Not to worry," Steven said, "we've got the rental again, parked out front."

She sighed with relief. "Thank God for that. Funny how that represents freedom. Away from here and my mother."

Reyes pointed out, "You might want to go a little easy on her right now."

"No, not right now, I'm too damn angry."

Steven wrapped an arm around her. "At least if this is anger, it blows off and disintegrates at the same time."

She looked at him and smiled. "Thank you for that. I didn't think I would ever smile again."

"You will, and you'll understand more as time goes on, and believe me. It will make it a little bit easier."

"Maybe," she muttered, "but right now I can't even begin to think about it."

Steven loaded the bags into the SUV and helped her and Reyes into their seats.

"What about the cops?" she asked.

"I'll be just a minute." Steven shot a look at Reyes. With some kind of mutual understanding shared, Steven turned and walked the twenty feet to where several cops stood by, waiting.

STEVEN GREETED THE men. "We're heading to a hotel for the night, after I get Reyes to a clinic to get that head checked out." He pulled out a card and a pen, wrote down the hotel number on it. "We'll be here for a few days. Opal doesn't feel comfortable around her mother right now, so best if we take her somewhere safe."

"With a mother like that, I would do the same," one officer muttered, accepting the card.

"If you need us or need Reyes to come down and make a statement, give us a couple days for that head of his to be checked out, then he can come in. Hopefully you won't need too much from Opal or me, but I do understand you'll have questions. Again, a couple days for her to rest will help her a lot."

The policemen nodded.

Steven shook their hands, then returned to the SUV, where Opal looked at him curiously.

"What was that all about?" she asked.

"All of us will need to go to the station and give statements," he murmured, "but not today and hopefully not tomorrow. I told them that I need to get Reyes to a clinic to get his head checked out, so that should give him a day or two. And, after seeing your face, Opal, everyone is willing to give you a bit of time too."

She slumped in place. "I forgot about needing to do that."

"I haven't," he said cheerfully, starting up the engine and driving past the cruiser, where they were opening the door for Ruby to get in. He glanced at Opal, only to see her staring straight ahead. Betrayal was hard but way worse when it came from those who were supposed to love you.

"Hey, thanks for that excuse," Reyes said from the back seat. "I'd be happy to have another day or two of rest before the inquisition starts. And the clinic is perfectly acceptable."

"And not an excuse." Steven chuckled, as he took several more turns. "Levi has arranged for Ice's father to take a look at your head."

"*Noooo*," Reyes wailed from the back seat. "I don't need a doctor."

Steven laughed, as he pulled up to the front of a large officious-looking building. "It doesn't matter if you do or not. You're going in." Then Steven gave a knowing look at Opal, but she immediately shook her head. "Oh no you don't. I'm not seeing the doctor. Reyes is."

"Hey, if I have to, you have to," Reyes said, with dark laughter coming from behind her.

She twisted in her seat. "I didn't get hit over the head twice."

He glared at her. "If you were a nice person, you

wouldn't keep bringing that up."

She laughed. "And, if you were a nice person, you wouldn't try to throw me to the wolves with you."

"Misery loves company."

Steven interrupted their witty banter. "Too bad. Both of you are getting the once-over." Steven pointed to the front door. "There is Ice's father, and he's waiting for us. He should have gone home a long time ago. Are you going to tell Levi that you wasted his father-in-law's time?"

"Shit." Reyes stared at the older man, clearly waiting for him. Reyes then opened the car door and slowly got out. "At least if I have to see someone, I get to see the best."

"Ditto," Opal said, as she slid out as well.

Steven walked up to the doctor and shook his hand. "Dr. Danning, thank you so much."

Dr. Danning waved away the thanks. "When Levi calls, I know he needs help. He's too damn independent to ask for a favor if it wasn't needed." The doctor's gaze went from one to the other. "Let's get you into an examining room. Levi really knows how to get his people in trouble, doesn't he?"

"Well, I've worked for Levi for a long time," Reyes muttered, "and I have a hard head."

"Stubborn to boot, I bet." The doctor laughed at the look on Reyes's face. "Let's get you both checked over."

Chapter 13

G ETTING CHECKED OUT took longer than anyone expected, as Dr. Danning was thorough.

By the time they returned to the vehicle, Reyes was moving slowly, and Opal wasn't doing much better. She watched Steven hop into the vehicle. As he pulled away, she asked, "Have we got a reservation somewhere?"

"We sure do, but honestly, I also need food."

"Me too," chimed in Reyes from the back seat. "I'm starving."

She laughed. "So where are we going then?"

"Now, to the hotel. First, we'll check in. Then we'll get some food. Our options are, we'll go out and grab a meal, or we'll get something from room service, or we could just bring something back for Reyes."

Reyes protested, "Hey, I'll be fine."

"Yeah," Opal said, "you are and certainly will be, but you can't be up and walking around with a lump that size. No way that is happening."

"I'm not used to being mothered," he admitted.

"You may not be used to it," Opal began, "but, if I call and tell your wife what happened, and she finds out you're not taking care—"

"No, no, no," he said hurriedly, "don't do that."

She chuckled. "Right, so accept the ministrations and

know that, as long as I can see you healing, I won't be too worried."

He chuckled, and that's what they did. They checked into the hotel, and she immediately inspected the adjoining rooms, then nodded. "This works." She didn't say anything about the fact that there was one bed for her and Steven.

In fact, it seemed to be the most natural thing in the world. She still didn't understand why it hadn't happened before. As far as she was concerned, they were destined to be partners, and she had always known that in the back of her mind, assuming that they would come together at another point in time—or might not, she didn't really know. But he was here now, and she wasn't letting him go.

With a promise to bring Reyes back some food, she and Steven stepped back out to the SUV. She asked him, "We're safe here, right?"

"Yes, we're safe." He held up his phone. "And I got confirmation from Levi that everybody named in that book has been picked up."

"Thank God for that." She beamed. "I wonder how long it will take before I stop looking over my shoulder?"

"Quite a while, and so it should be after a traumatic incident and injuries like that." He smiled, as he tucked her hand into his arm. "We want to know that you'll take as many precautions as you can and that you'll be smart every time you step out the door."

"That's a given now," she admitted. Then, with a smile, she added, "Thank you."

"You're welcome," he said, with a laugh. "Now, what do you want for food?"

"I want food, but you're the connoisseur and the one who eats mega amounts, so you tell me."

"So, any place is good?" When she nodded, he asked, "Seafood?"

She thought about it and then nodded. "Yeah, seafood sounds good." With that, he punched it into the GPS, and they were off, heading to a restaurant. Luckily it was a weekday, and they didn't have any trouble with reservations, so they got in right away. As she was seated, she looked around. "It seems almost impossible to imagine doing something normal like this again."

"Yet it is," he noted. "And honestly, I'm surprised that you even agreed to come out, with your face still healing."

At that reminder, she stopped and whispered, "Oh my God, I forgot." Then he started to laugh and laugh. She stared at him in horror, her hands going to her face. "You should have reminded me."

He chuckled. "Honestly, it looks puffy at this point. You're beautiful. So forget about it."

She stared at him. "No way in hell I'll believe that. I saw my face not very long ago today, when I was packing up. It's so ugly."

"I don't agree. As far as I'm concerned, you're beautiful, no matter what."

She looked at him and nodded. "You would say that. I wonder why we didn't end up together before."

"I don't know. Maybe it wasn't the right time." He chuckled. "I was kind of an ass back then anyway, but together definitely is an option now." He squeezed her hand gently. "It depends on what you want. You've been through an awful lot."

"I'm in," she said immediately, "and I couldn't be happier about it. Honestly, it feels right. As if we've always been together."

He smiled at her. "Me too. Are you planning on staying here?"

"I don't know what I'm doing." She stared at him. "Why?"

"I was planning on going to Texas."

Her eyebrows shot up. She hadn't considered that, but she loved the idea of getting away. Creating a fresh start somewhere. "Back to Levi?"

He nodded. "Yeah, I've been looking for a change. I've spent so much time in California that I was ready to try something new for a change."

She nodded slowly. "I'll have to try rearranging my veterinarian training. Different states have different requirements, might have to redo courses—or take new ones."

"I'm sure you can work that out."

"Maybe," she agreed. "I need to sort that out soon anyway. Changing states will complicate things though."

"And now that everybody has been picked up, you can tell the truth," he reminded her. "There won't be any issue fixing this now."

She winced at that. "I guess, but that's a tale I don't want to begin to explain."

"I do know a few places where you could get another practicum, where Levi also has a lot of connections too."

"But would it mean starting all over again?" she asked.

"How long do you have left?"

"A month."

Steven nodded. "Maybe when we talk to them, you can explain what happened, then somebody could come up with a solution."

"I hope so."

"For now, let's deal with what we can deal with." And that appeared to be dinner. Very quickly they were served huge platters of pasta, with fresh prawns all over the top, smothered in a lemony cream sauce.

"Wow," she said, "this looks delicious." It also was a massive serving for her, but she also was quite confident that, if she couldn't eat it all, then Steven would. By the time she finished half her plate, she realized she was full, but he was still going strong. She sat back and reached for a piece of garlic bread. When she watched him eat, a smile came on her lips. Then deciding now was better than later, she murmured, "You didn't say anything about the sleeping arrangements."

"Nope, whatever you want is fine with me." He forked in a bite of pasta and eyed her closely.

She chuckled. "That's good because I want you in my arms and in my bed," she stated flat-out. "And I don't want to beat around the bush about it or waste any more time." He slowly lowered his fork and studied her. She nodded. "Don't make it seem as if you're surprised." She chuckled at the expression on his face.

"I'm not surprised at anything except the approach." He flashed her a wicked grin.

"I feel as if I've already suffered enough, and I don't want to anymore," she murmured sadly. "So anything that works to make me feel better right now, I'll take it. So, if it helps me to forget, all the better. I'm still in shock over my mother's behavior."

"I'm sorry for your sake."

"I think Reyes should sue her for what she did to him— or the cops should charge her."

"Can you deal with her facing assault charges?" he asked,

looking at her. "Seriously?"

She sighed. "Maybe not, but it's not fair what she did to him."

"It isn't, and I'm not sure what to do about it, but I'll leave it up to the police. Don't forget the police reached out to confirm your family's safety, only to find out Ruby had hit Reyes and had left the scene. Marshal too. That will go into their reports. I don't know how that will be resolved."

She nodded. "It's so infuriating."

He grinned at her. "I'm glad to hear you say that. You always have been a defender of the innocent."

"It doesn't feel as if I'm a defender of anything right now. It feels as if my mother took advantage ... of so many things. I find myself wondering how much of it was because of the damn diamond. Things like diamonds can make people stupid."

"I know. I know." When his phone buzzed, Steven checked it and nodded. "That's Reyes. He heard back from Di."

"And who is Di?"

He laughed. "That's Dezi's partner, another of Levi's men. Her full name is Diamond, but she's brilliant, also a jeweler. And she says the value of that diamond is well over ten million."

Her jaw dropped, as she stared at him. "Oh my God," she cried out softly, then looked around quickly to make sure they couldn't be overheard.

"Right." He smiled. "So take that into account, when you think about your mother's behavior."

"Got it." She leaned forward and whispered, "Is Di interested in it?"

"I don't know. Do you want to find out?"

"Maybe, but we'll have to get it appraised properly."

"What would you do with the money?"

She shook her head. "I don't even know." She winced and then reluctantly added, "I might give some to my mother." He stared at her, with a knowing smile. She shrugged. "I don't even know what to say right now."

"So don't make any decisions right now," he said calmly. "When you're a little more recovered from all this, you'll make more informed decisions."

"Maybe." But it was hard to believe. That was one hell of an inheritance.

"Obviously you still have a degree of sympathy for your mother."

"I know what we went through," she explained, "and it was brutal. The media, the cops, the investigations, the public, it was beyond painful. It changes us. I just need some time."

"Understood," he agreed. He finished his meal, then looked over at her and asked, "Are you ready to go?"

She nodded, "Yeah, but what about Reyes?" Just then the waitress delivered a take-out bag for them. She frowned at it. "I don't remember you ordering that."

He chuckled. "Hey, you've been a little busy, with other things on your mind."

"Yeah, ya think?" As they hopped up, he wrapped an arm around her, pulled her close, dropping a kiss on the top of her head. "Come on. Let's head out. Next stop should be a nap for you."

"I hope not," she said, with feeling. When he turned to her, she shook her head. "Now, if you think for one moment that you're sleeping tonight, you're wrong."

A wicked grin flashed across his face. "Sweetheart, you

can call the shots tonight. If you don't want to sleep, we don't have to sleep."

"I'm not sleeping," she said instantly. "I've had enough of this. I've also had enough of being a victim, and I've had enough of people keeping all these secrets from me and doing shit behind my back. Promise me that you'll never lie to me."

"No problem," he said. "I promise. Lying has never been my thing."

"I know," she stated. "That's why I believe you. It's just that it hurts so much to think about what my mother did and how she's been feeling all this time. That her focus has been her future, not mine—if I even have one."

"And yet you also understand that ... at least to some degree."

"I understand it, and that just makes me angrier," she muttered. He drove back to the hotel, and she had to admit that she was completely overwhelmed with joy when she saw Reyes was still up, sitting there. He looked over, smiled. "See? I'm fine."

"I'm glad to hear that," she said, "but remember? I've got your wife on speed dial." When his eyes widened in horror, she laughed. "See? I can play games like the best of them."

"And yet games aren't really your thing," Reyes murmured gently. "So don't change. Just heal and move on, but don't ever change."

She smiled at him, then walked over and gave him a gentle kiss on the cheek. "You're a nice man, Reyes."

When he gasped in horror, she chuckled, then turned and walked to the bedroom. She called back to Steven, "I'll take a quick shower."

With that, she headed to the bathroom and tried to wash off the stench of the day and of her life. She couldn't even imagine that everything she'd found out over the last few days was all because of Steven. She had known on some level that he would always be there for her. She didn't know why it had taken her so damn long to get in touch. Maybe it was all about timing. Maybe it was all about fate. Maybe it was so much more than anybody could even explain. She didn't know, but, as she stepped out of the shower and wrapped herself in a towel, she felt 100 percent better.

When he walked into the bathroom, with a towel around his waist, she grinned and felt wonderful. She opened her arms and asked, "Shower first or later?"

"How about both?" He ushered her right back under the steaming water, pulling loose her towel and dropping his, then wrapping his arms around her, pulling her up against his heated body.

"God," she cried out, squirming against him. "I've wanted to do this right from the beginning."

He laughed and said, "Liar."

"No, not really," she agreed. "First, I wanted hugs and cuddles, and then I wanted every damn kiss you had to give."

"Well, you didn't want to sleep tonight, so I'm here to make sure that doesn't happen." And, when he lowered his head, she believed him. A half hour later, when he lifted her body, her trembling and aching body, throbbing with need, against the shower wall to plunge deep within, she believed him.

When he dried her off, picked her up, carried her to the bed, and made love to her all over again, she believed him.

Somewhere around three o'clock in the morning, she rolled over on top of him and whispered, "I'm still awake."

"And that's what you wanted," he reminded her, as he cupped her breasts, holding and cuddling her gently. "You call it."

"More, make me forget." And, with that, he once again took her to the edges of passion and carried her over. When she sank back down on the other side of more orgasms, she whispered, "Okay, now it's time for sleep."

"Are you sure?" he murmured in a teasing voice, nuzzling her neck. "I can keep this up, if I need to."

"I'm sure you can," she whispered, her voice soft and gentle, on the verge of exhaustion. "In the morning we can pick it up."

But when she woke up in the morning with nothing but nightmares consuming her, his warm hands stroked her skin, his tender kisses soothed her skin, and then finally a demanding mouth wrapped around her nipple, pulling her from the nightmares, and made her body throb, and she cried out for more.

When she came crashing back down on the other side, she stared at him. "Is that your remedy for nightmares?"

"Yeah, you got a problem with that?" he asked, with a gentle grin.

"No." She winked at him. "However, if that's how I'll wake up, I might not be so terrified to go to sleep."

He burst out laughing. "Why don't we put it to the test? You sleep," he said, "and, if you have another nightmare, I'll make sure I wake you up in a nice way."

And, with that, she did crash and soon was sound asleep again. And, when the nightmares hit her again, he once again woke her up, and she started to believe in miracles.

By the time she woke up much later that morning, with several hours of actual sleep, he was sitting beside her, a smile on his face.

"What time is it?" she asked.

"It's ten," he said gently, "and, no, you don't have to move."

"Don't we have to leave?"

"No, no check-out today." He stroked a finger down her cheek. "I've booked us for another day."

"You better have booked Reyes too." She rolled over to stare up at him. "How is he?"

"Oh, I have, and he needs another day before he flies. You have to be careful with head injuries and flying."

She went quietly contemplative, then smiled. "I think you might have done it," she murmured.

"Done what?" he asked, looking at her questioningly.

"Broke me of the nightmares. I don't remember sleeping this well in a very long time."

"Are you sure? Because if you need to give that another try, I'm totally up for it." And, with that, he picked up her hand, placed it down on his body.

She knew immediately that he was totally up for anything she wanted. She smiled at him. "We're going to have fun, aren't we?"

"We sure will," he murmured, as he slid down flat on the bed and wrapped his hands around her hips, pulling her close. "I'm so glad you're back in my life."

"I think I've always been in your life. We just had to find each other again."

He smiled, and, just before his lips took hers, he whispered, "Guess what? I found you, and I'm never letting you go."

Epilogue

LEVI STOOD BEHIND Ice, his hands wrapped around her waist, as he held her close and surveyed the massive compound they had built together. They were up on the roof, with glasses of wine and a bottle beside them, surveying the landscape.

"I can't believe all we've done," she murmured. "Everything we've accomplished, the networking we've built, the friends, the families." She turned around to give him a kiss on the jaw. "Nice job there, Daddy."

"Nice job yourself, Mommy," he said, chuckling.

"I didn't think we'd ever get here," she admitted.

"Neither did I," he agreed. "With everything we've gone through, there were days I wasn't sure it was even safe to try."

"Understood, but, in spite of it all, I think we did good."

"We did, indeed," he murmured. "Now the question is, do you want to keep doing what we're doing, or do you want to find something else to do with this life of ours?"

"I don't know," she said truthfully. "Obviously our lives have changed, things have changed, and the people in them have certainly changed, yet I can't imagine doing anything very different from what we've always done," she explained. "It feels as if this is us, you know? As if this is who we are."

"That's because it *is* who we are." Levi cuddled her closer. "That still doesn't mean we can't do something different too."

She nodded against his chest, her long blond hair softly moving in the breeze, something that he'd always absolutely adored about her. And even though she knew her long hair could be a weapon used against her, she kept it because it mattered to both of them, and he loved her for that.

Levi appreciated how Ice made allowances when there were allowances to be made, how she made concessions when concessions needed to be made, and how she stood in the face of everything, every wrongdoing in the world, knowing that she had the ability to enact change where it needed to be enacted.

He had never loved anybody more than he loved her and never more than he did at this moment.

Ice looked up at him and looped her arms around his neck. "I think we better keep doing what we're doing, since we're just so good at it. Yet I think we should do it a little differently. Do more with Bullard and maybe Terkel—if he ever gets that nightmare sorted out. He's damn good at what he does, but that mess he's in ..."

Levi burst out laughing, leaned over, and kissed her gently.

"But ..." she hesitated, then the words rushed out. "I might want another baby." When he stared at her in shock, she giggled. "Surely three is not too many."

"I don't know," he protested mockingly. "They're quite the little horrors."

"We have two sons, and I want a daughter."

"You know we can't control that," he warned.

"No"—she grinned wisely—"but I can keep trying until I get what I want." She pulled his head down. "Besides, we have such fun trying."

And he couldn't argue with that. As a matter of fact, he'd never been able to argue with her over anything important. She was his wife. She was his heart, and she was his life.

This concludes Book 29 of Heroes for Hire: Steven's Solace.

Terk's Guardians: Radar (Book #1)

Having cultivated his instincts through years of naval missions, Radar is roaming the world, working part-time for Levi and Bullard. When he's instructed to go to Paris to help out a new start-up, he's not sure what to expect. Especially given the caginess of Levi's description of those who Radar would be working for. Outside of telling him, *He'd fit right in*, there is minimal intel on the job itself. Plus Radar's working with two men he doesn't know, and they aren't willing to share their own secrets.

Sammy threw in her heart and soul to help her best friend and fellow hacker track down a bomber, who'd left devastation behind on the Parisian streets over the last few years. When they finally get something tangible, they contact the authorities to help. That's when Sammy's world goes to hell.

The race to save Sammy—and, indeed, Paris from an imminent attack—has Radar questioning his own instincts, and the abilities of those around him. … especially Sammy's.

I T HAD BEEN weeks since the chaotic mass wedding and the biggest party that Terkel had ever attended in his life. That it was all for him and his friends and his team had filled his heart with joy and had reminded him what was important in life. Now, as he eyed his wife's protruding belly, Terk realized that they still had a ton more work to do— turning this old castle outside of London into their team's new headquarters. He looked over at Gage. "We need to do an assessment of what still needs to happen here in the next little bit."

"We're also getting calls for help." Gage frowned, then said, "I wasn't going to mention it, but he's called twice today already."

"Who?"

"Johan. He wants to talk to you."

"What does he want?" Terk asked.

Gage shook his head. "I've been pushing him off because I know, as soon as I call him back, our free time here will come to an end."

"It will change for sure," Terk murmured. "We can't get out of that."

"I know. I know," Gage admitted. "I was still trying though."

Terk burst into laughter, nodding. "It's been pretty special. Crazy at times, with all this work on the place and all. It seems even those who left after the weddings are back today."

"And that will change things too," Gage noted.

Even as they talked, Damon and Tasha walked in the door, all smiles and hugs.

"You guys look great," Terkel said.

"You should try getting away every once in a while," Damon suggested.

"And I would, but, right now, this place is still a nightmare." Terk shrugged.

Damon raised his eyebrows, as he looked around. "It's looking phenomenal."

"We're getting there," Terk acknowledged. "We're not quite there yet, but we're close." Then he studied the newlyweds, smiled, and asked, "Are you guys ready to get back to work?"

Damon and Tasha both nodded. "Yeah, it was good to get away, but honestly we missed you guys," Tasha said, as she walked over and gave Terk a big hug. "And now, after confirming that I'm pregnant, I'm so excited. I really just want to be home with family."

Damon nodded. "Even when I told her that we could stay longer, she was like, *Nope, I want to go home*," he said, with a big smile.

"So, that's where we're at, and that's good," Terkel replied, "because you really do want to know who your friends are and where you'll be in these times to come."

"Exactly," Tasha stated. "And, with that, I'm heading upstairs. I might even have a nap." She laughed, rolling her eyes, and quickly disappeared.

"She hasn't quite adjusted to the fact that she has zero energy. And it's still early in her pregnancy," Damon shared. "So she's not sure what that means."

"It means she's pregnant," Celia declared, as she waddled into the kitchen.

Damon took one look at her and winced. "My God, I sure hope Tasha is not carrying twins."

Celia chuckled. "I have no clue what she's carrying. And, right now, it's all I can do to keep my own world somewhat contained."

Damon nodded. "I hear you there," he murmured. "So what's going on?"

Terk replied, "Johan is being insistent this morning. He's called a couple times already." Just then, Terkel checked his phone. "I had mine off," he confessed. Reluctantly he turned it back on, and it rang immediately. "Well, here we go." He frowned, switching it to Speaker. "Johan, what's up?"

"Don't you guys ever answer your phones?" he asked in exasperation.

"Sorry, mine was off," Terk stated. "What can I do for you?"

"What you can do for us is give us some help," he snapped. "We have two escaped prisoners."

"More escaped prisoners?" Terk asked in a drawling voice.

"Hey, they were being transported from France," he clarified, "and now the shit's hit the fan."

"Who are these prisoners?"

"They're wanted by Interpol, but we had first crack to prosecute them, so they were being transported," he said. "However, on the ferry, somehow they escaped."

"Did they go via the Chunnel or the ferry?"

"Yeah, we're still trying to get the details on all that," Johan replied. "I'm sending over the information I have right now. We really need these guys, and we need them back now."

"And why are you calling us?" Terk asked.

At that question, Johan sighed. "Because there's a problem."

"What kind of problem?"

"We weren't supposed to have them in the first place,"

he shared reluctantly. "So none of this can come back to us."

"Great, so we're supposed to do a catch-and-retrieve mission, and you don't want anybody to know you guys did the original catch?"

"Not only can they *not* know that these guys were coming to us, no one can know that you were hired by us. So I hope you guys have your banking set up because we have the budget to pay you."

When he named the figure, everybody in the room was stunned, and they just stared at each other, their eyebrows sky-high. An audible silence took over, as they contemplated the monies involved.

"Fifty percent now, fifty percent when you bring them in," Johan confirmed. "I can't tell you how important it is for your future possibility of working with us if you can do this. ... If you can't? Well, I can't guarantee too much more work."

"Send us what you've got," Terkel said, "and I'll see who I've got available."

"If you don't have anybody available because you're all still sitting around in whatever marital-bliss thing you guys have going on over there, not to mention the baby factory," he added, with a snort, "you need to hire somebody."

"Oh, I definitely need to hire several somebodies." Terk groaned. "Still I wouldn't send them out on a mission all alone," he stated, knowing that, when working previously for the US government, Terk's team had always been the intel gatherers, the secret weapon in the background, not necessarily the front-runners. "We must ensure they're good enough to even go on a job in our name."

"That's your problem," Johan declared. "You have literally four hours to get back to me. Well, no, you *had* four, but now you only have one. You would have had longer, but you didn't answer your damn phone." And, with that, Johan disconnected.

Terk addressed the group, "You heard the figures."

"Yeah, we sure did," Gage said, "and we definitely need the money for our own satellite, so I'm willing." He looked around at the others. "Who's coming with me?"

Calum spoke up. "And that's the problem. We normally work as a team. Two to four of us. Now it's a whole different ball game. Are we doing this alone or what?" Calum asked. "Do you think this is a two-man job or four?"

"Even if four, we can't leave this place unprotected," Terk noted. "An awful lot of very important people are here. ... So we need a plan in place. However, let's not forgot that we have two other teams who we work with as well."

"Right." Calum nodded. "Levi and Bullard, correct? But, if that's the case, and we need help this time, then they must send men to London or Paris, just to be local for this job. So maybe save their men for the next job?"

Terk frowned, contemplating that logistics issue. He pulled out his phone and pressed a speed dial number. "Levi, do you have anyone close to us?"

"I know of some over there," Levi said cautiously. "Why are you asking?"

"Johan has a job for us, but we're hardly set up with the manpower yet."

"That is something we need to sort out. I could have someone at your place in a few days—if you're set up for team members moving in?"

"If you know anyone available today, call me. Otherwise send this guy," Terk replied abruptly. "We'll find room regardless. If we can pull off this job, I suspect we'll get very busy, very quickly." With that he disconnected and looked around at the group. "I was contacted by someone not too long ago," he shared, checking his phone. "It's one of the reasons I had turned this off, so I could think about it. Anyway, his name is Riff, and I used to know him, and he sent out the word that he was looking for work," Terkel explained. "I just wasn't sure that we were ready to hire anybody."

"Probably not, but, if we'll be taking MI6 jobs," Damon suggested, "we need more people, particularly given the pregnancies right now."

"I agree," Terk stated. "I just didn't want to start down that road so soon. I was hoping to have, say, a half-dozen men from Levi and Ice, and, if we were so lucky, the same from Bullard. But that means additional housing, cooks, weapons, etc. And we're not there yet."

"I don't think we have a choice," Damon pointed out quietly. "What's the deal with this Riff guy, the possible new hire?"

Before Terk could respond, Wade stepped forward. "I know him. … He was always a little different."

"He's definitely a little different," Terkel confirmed, "because his abilities are a little different."

"He has abilities?" Damon stared at Terk in delight. "So how come you haven't hired him before?"

"A couple reasons. Before, he couldn't pass muster with the CIA."

"Why was that?" Damon asked.

"Because he was once suspected in a murder case, and they steer clear of that messiness."

"Ouch, whose murder?" Gage asked.

"His fiancée's," Terk said.

"And did he kill her?"

"No, he didn't," Terk replied, "but it affected him badly."

"Yeah, you're not kidding," Gage stated. "Can you imagine? Not only dealing with the grief and the loss but you also have to deal with the rest of the world suspecting you."

"Exactly." Terk nodded. "I know he didn't do it, and he knows he didn't do it, but it's really a matter of whether any of you will have an issue with it."

"If you trust him, I'm willing to give Riff a try," Damon said. "Send him out with me. I'll put him through the wringer."

"One more thing," Terkel added, "and it's one of the reasons Riff called me in the first place. He'll be looking for help as well."

"What kind of help?" Damon asked.

"He still hasn't found out who killed his fiancée," Terk replied. "As you can imagine, he needs to resolve that issue, before he can move on." Just then his phone buzzed. *Levi.* "That was fast," Terk said, with a smile.

"Radar is in Paris. I called him. Give the word, and he's yours. He was doing a job in Africa, then headed to Paris to see some family."

"We want him," Terk said immediately, walking over to a whiteboard, full of house renovations in progress. He grabbed a corner and started writing. "Give me his contact information. I'll set it up."

"And Ice will invoice you for him," Levi replied, laughing. "This will work out well for all of us."

"Ha," Terk muttered. "Says you. We need our shit here operational, and I wouldn't have said we were there yet."

"Doesn't matter. You'll learn on the fly." And, with that, Levi shared Radar's information, signing off with, "He's waiting for you."

Terk stared down at his phone, then lifted his gaze to his team. "Thoughts?"

"Radar, Riff, and me," Gage said immediately. "Damon too, if need be." Gage looked at the others. "Unless anyone has something to say about Riff?" With nobody objecting, Gage added, "Still, if we can't widen our base, we'll have to send out one to two new men on each and every job. Although, if Riff comes to work with us, he comes with conditions. We'd have to foot the bill for that."

"If Riff comes to work for us, of course we would help him solve his own matter too," Wade confirmed. "I say, give Riff a call, and let's get started. And, while you're working with Riff, maybe get the information on his fiancée's murder, so we can start researching the details and possibly get this sorted quickly, after this catch-and-retrieve is completed."

Terkel nodded. "Any objections?" he asked, but there were none. "Okay then, I'll give Riff a call, and one of you call Johan. Tell him that, if he's got that kind of money sitting around, we have no problem taking it off his hands." Then with a big fat grin, he said, "Looks like we're in business, ladies and gents."

"We still need a company name though," Wade reminded him.

"And I have one." Terk hesitated. "It's partly from this castle. Above the door in Latin, roughly translated, it says, *In times of war, ... we guard.*"

The others looked at him in surprise.

"I was thinking, *Guardian Security.*"

"And for short, ... because you know it'll happen"—Wade gave a fat grin—"Terk's Guardians."

Find Radar (Book #1) here!

To find out more visit Dale Mayer's website.

https://geni.us/DMRadarUniversal

Author's Note

Thank you for reading Steven's Solace: Heroes for Hire, Book 29! If you enjoyed the book, please take a moment and leave a short review.

Dear reader,

I love to hear from readers, and you can contact me at my website: www.dalemayer.com or at my Facebook author page. To be informed of new releases and special offers, sign up for my newsletter or follow me on BookBub. And if you are interested in joining Dale Mayer's Reader Group, here is the Facebook sign up page.
http://geni.us/DaleMayerFBGroup

Cheers,
Dale Mayer

Your THREE Free Books Are Waiting!

Grab your copy of SEALs of Honor Books 1 – 3 for free!

Meet Mason, Hawk and Dane. *Brave, badass warriors who serve their country with honor and love their women to the limits of life and death.*

DOWNLOAD your copy right now! Just tell me where to send it.

dalemayer.com/seals-honor-free-bundle

About the Author

Dale Mayer is a *USA Today* best-selling author, best known for her SEALs military romances, her Psychic Visions series, and her Lovely Lethal Garden cozy series. Her contemporary romances are raw and full of passion and emotion (Broken But ... Mending, Hathaway House series). Her thrillers will keep you guessing (Kate Morgan, By Death series), and her romantic comedies will keep you giggling (*It's a Dog's Life*, a stand-alone novella; and the Broken Protocols series, starring Charming Marvin, the cat).

Dale honors the stories that come to her—and some of them are crazy, break all the rules and cross multiple genres!

To go with her fiction, she also writes nonfiction in many different fields, with books available on résumé writing, companion gardening, and the US mortgage system. All her books are available in print and ebook format.

Connect with Dale Mayer Online

Dale's Website – www.dalemayer.com

Twitter – @DaleMayer

Facebook Page – geni.us/DaleMayerFBFanPage

Facebook Group – geni.us/DaleMayerFBGroup

BookBub – geni.us/DaleMayerBookbub

Instagram – geni.us/DaleMayerInstagram

Goodreads – geni.us/DaleMayerGoodreads

Newsletter – geni.us/DaleNews

Also by Dale Mayer

Published Adult Books:

Shadow Recon
Magnus, Book 1
Rogan, Book 2
Egan, Book 3
Barret, Book 4

Bullard's Battle
Ryland's Reach, Book 1
Cain's Cross, Book 2
Eton's Escape, Book 3
Garret's Gambit, Book 4
Kano's Keep, Book 5
Fallon's Flaw, Book 6
Quinn's Quest, Book 7
Bullard's Beauty, Book 8
Bullard's Best, Book 9
Bullard's Battle, Books 1–2
Bullard's Battle, Books 3–4
Bullard's Battle, Books 5–6
Bullard's Battle, Books 7–8

Terkel's Team

Damon's Deal, Book 1

Wade's War, Book 2

Gage's Goal, Book 3

Calum's Contact, Book 4

Rick's Road, Book 5

Scott's Summit, Book 6

Brody's Beast, Book 7

Terkel's Twist, Book 8

Terkel's Triumph, Book 9

Terk's Guardians

Radar, Book 1

Kate Morgan

Simon Says... Hide, Book 1

Simon Says... Jump, Book 2

Simon Says... Ride, Book 3

Simon Says... Scream, Book 4

Simon Says... Run, Book 5

Simon Says... Walk, Book 6

Simon Says... Forgive, Book 7

Hathaway House

Aaron, Book 1

Brock, Book 2

Cole, Book 3

Denton, Book 4

Elliot, Book 5

Finn, Book 6

Gregory, Book 7

Heath, Book 8

Iain, Book 9

Jaden, Book 10

Keith, Book 11

Lance, Book 12

Melissa, Book 13

Nash, Book 14

Owen, Book 15

Percy, Book 16

Quinton, Book 17

Ryatt, Book 18

Spencer, Book 19

Timothy, Book 20

Hathaway House, Books 1–3

Hathaway House, Books 4–6

Hathaway House, Books 7–9

The K9 Files

Ethan, Book 1

Pierce, Book 2

Zane, Book 3

Blaze, Book 4

Lucas, Book 5

Parker, Book 6

Carter, Book 7

Weston, Book 8

Greyson, Book 9

Rowan, Book 10

Caleb, Book 11

Kurt, Book 12

Tucker, Book 13

Harley, Book 14

Kyron, Book 15

Jenner, Book 16

Rhys, Book 17

Landon, Book 18

Harper, Book 19

Kascius, Book 20

Declan, Book 21

The K9 Files, Books 1–2

The K9 Files, Books 3–4

The K9 Files, Books 5–6

The K9 Files, Books 7–8

The K9 Files, Books 9–10

The K9 Files, Books 11–12

Lovely Lethal Gardens

Arsenic in the Azaleas, Book 1

Bones in the Begonias, Book 2

Corpse in the Carnations, Book 3

Daggers in the Dahlias, Book 4

Evidence in the Echinacea, Book 5

Footprints in the Ferns, Book 6

Gun in the Gardenias, Book 7

Handcuffs in the Heather, Book 8

Ice Pick in the Ivy, Book 9

Jewels in the Juniper, Book 10

Killer in the Kiwis, Book 11

Lifeless in the Lilies, Book 12

Murder in the Marigolds, Book 13

Nabbed in the Nasturtiums, Book 14

Offed in the Orchids, Book 15

Poison in the Pansies, Book 16

Quarry in the Quince, Book 17

Revenge in the Roses, Book 18

Silenced in the Sunflowers, Book 19

Toes up in the Tulips, Book 20

Uzi in the Urn, Book 21

Victim in the Violets, Book 22

Lovely Lethal Gardens, Books 1–2

Lovely Lethal Gardens, Books 3–4

Lovely Lethal Gardens, Books 5–6

Lovely Lethal Gardens, Books 7–8

Lovely Lethal Gardens, Books 9–10

Psychic Visions Series

Tuesday's Child

Hide 'n Go Seek

Maddy's Floor

Garden of Sorrow

Knock Knock...

Rare Find

Eyes to the Soul

Now You See Her

Shattered

Into the Abyss
Seeds of Malice
Eye of the Falcon
Itsy-Bitsy Spider
Unmasked
Deep Beneath
From the Ashes
Stroke of Death
Ice Maiden
Snap, Crackle…
What If…
Talking Bones
String of Tears
Inked Forever
Psychic Visions Books 1–3
Psychic Visions Books 4–6
Psychic Visions Books 7–9

By Death Series
Touched by Death
Haunted by Death
Chilled by Death
By Death Books 1–3

Broken Protocols – Romantic Comedy Series
Cat's Meow
Cat's Pajamas
Cat's Cradle
Cat's Claus

Broken Protocols 1-4

Broken and... Mending
Skin

Scars

Scales (of Justice)

Broken but… Mending 1-3

Glory
Genesis

Tori

Celeste

Glory Trilogy

Biker Blues
Morgan: Biker Blues, Volume 1

Cash: Biker Blues, Volume 2

SEALs of Honor
Mason: SEALs of Honor, Book 1

Hawk: SEALs of Honor, Book 2

Dane: SEALs of Honor, Book 3

Swede: SEALs of Honor, Book 4

Shadow: SEALs of Honor, Book 5

Cooper: SEALs of Honor, Book 6

Markus: SEALs of Honor, Book 7

Evan: SEALs of Honor, Book 8

Mason's Wish: SEALs of Honor, Book 9

Chase: SEALs of Honor, Book 10

Brett: SEALs of Honor, Book 11

Devlin: SEALs of Honor, Book 12

Easton: SEALs of Honor, Book 13

Ryder: SEALs of Honor, Book 14

Macklin: SEALs of Honor, Book 15

Corey: SEALs of Honor, Book 16

Warrick: SEALs of Honor, Book 17

Tanner: SEALs of Honor, Book 18

Jackson: SEALs of Honor, Book 19

Kanen: SEALs of Honor, Book 20

Nelson: SEALs of Honor, Book 21

Taylor: SEALs of Honor, Book 22

Colton: SEALs of Honor, Book 23

Troy: SEALs of Honor, Book 24

Axel: SEALs of Honor, Book 25

Baylor: SEALs of Honor, Book 26

Hudson: SEALs of Honor, Book 27

Lachlan: SEALs of Honor, Book 28

Paxton: SEALs of Honor, Book 29

Bronson: SEALs of Honor, Book 30

Hale: SEALs of Honor, Book 31

SEALs of Honor, Books 1–3

SEALs of Honor, Books 4–6

SEALs of Honor, Books 7–10

SEALs of Honor, Books 11–13

SEALs of Honor, Books 14–16

SEALs of Honor, Books 17–19

SEALs of Honor, Books 20–22

SEALs of Honor, Books 23–25

Heroes for Hire

Levi's Legend: Heroes for Hire, Book 1

Stone's Surrender: Heroes for Hire, Book 2

Merk's Mistake: Heroes for Hire, Book 3

Rhodes's Reward: Heroes for Hire, Book 4

Flynn's Firecracker: Heroes for Hire, Book 5

Logan's Light: Heroes for Hire, Book 6

Harrison's Heart: Heroes for Hire, Book 7

Saul's Sweetheart: Heroes for Hire, Book 8

Dakota's Delight: Heroes for Hire, Book 9

Tyson's Treasure: Heroes for Hire, Book 10

Jace's Jewel: Heroes for Hire, Book 11

Rory's Rose: Heroes for Hire, Book 12

Brandon's Bliss: Heroes for Hire, Book 13

Liam's Lily: Heroes for Hire, Book 14

North's Nikki: Heroes for Hire, Book 15

Anders's Angel: Heroes for Hire, Book 16

Reyes's Raina: Heroes for Hire, Book 17

Dezi's Diamond: Heroes for Hire, Book 18

Vince's Vixen: Heroes for Hire, Book 19

Ice's Icing: Heroes for Hire, Book 20

Johan's Joy: Heroes for Hire, Book 21

Galen's Gemma: Heroes for Hire, Book 22

Zack's Zest: Heroes for Hire, Book 23

Bonaparte's Belle: Heroes for Hire, Book 24

Noah's Nemesis: Heroes for Hire, Book 25

Tomas's Trials: Heroes for Hire, Book 26

Carson's Choice: Heroes for Hire, Book 27

Dante's Decision: Heroes for Hire, Book 28

Steven's Solace: Heroes for Hire, Book 29

Heroes for Hire, Books 1–3

Heroes for Hire, Books 4–6

Heroes for Hire, Books 7–9

Heroes for Hire, Books 10–12

Heroes for Hire, Books 13–15

Heroes for Hire, Books 16–18

Heroes for Hire, Books 19–21

Heroes for Hire, Books 22–24

SEALs of Steel

Badger: SEALs of Steel, Book 1

Erick: SEALs of Steel, Book 2

Cade: SEALs of Steel, Book 3

Talon: SEALs of Steel, Book 4

Laszlo: SEALs of Steel, Book 5

Geir: SEALs of Steel, Book 6

Jager: SEALs of Steel, Book 7

The Final Reveal: SEALs of Steel, Book 8

SEALs of Steel, Books 1–4

SEALs of Steel, Books 5–8

SEALs of Steel, Books 1–8

The Mavericks

Kerrick, Book 1

Griffin, Book 2

Jax, Book 3

Beau, Book 4

Asher, Book 5

Ryker, Book 6

Miles, Book 7

Nico, Book 8

Keane, Book 9

Lennox, Book 10

Gavin, Book 11

Shane, Book 12

Diesel, Book 13

Jerricho, Book 14

Killian, Book 15

Hatch, Book 16

Corbin, Book 17

Aiden, Book 18

The Mavericks, Books 1–2

The Mavericks, Books 3–4

The Mavericks, Books 5–6

The Mavericks, Books 7–8

The Mavericks, Books 9–10

The Mavericks, Books 11–12

Standalone Novellas

It's a Dog's Life

Riana's Revenge

Second Chances

Published Young Adult Books:

Family Blood Ties Series

Vampire in Denial

Vampire in Distress

Vampire in Design

Vampire in Deceit

Vampire in Defiance

Vampire in Conflict

Vampire in Chaos

Vampire in Crisis

Vampire in Control

Vampire in Charge

Family Blood Ties Set 1–3

Family Blood Ties Set 1–5

Family Blood Ties Set 4–6

Family Blood Ties Set 7–9

Sian's Solution, A Family Blood Ties Series Prequel
    Novelette

Design series

Dangerous Designs

Deadly Designs

Darkest Designs

Design Series Trilogy

Standalone

In Cassie's Corner

Gem Stone (a Gemma Stone Mystery)

Published Non-Fiction Books:

Career Essentials

Career Essentials: The Résumé

Career Essentials: The Cover Letter

Career Essentials: The Interview

Career Essentials: 3 in 1

Made in United States
Orlando, FL
05 June 2023

33834656R00137